DEATH IN THE HOUSE OF RAIN

1

Paul Halter books from Locked Room International:
The Lord of Misrule (2010)
The Fourth Door (2011)
The Seven Wonders of Crime (2011)
The Demon of Dartmoor (2012)
The Seventh Hypothesis (2012)
The Tiger's Head (2013)
The Crimson Fog (2013)
(Publisher's Weekly Top Mystery 2013 List)
The Night of the Wolf (short story collection 2013)
The Invisible Circle (2014)
The Picture from the Past (2014)
The Phantom Passage (2015)
Death Invites You (2016)
The Vampire Tree (2016)
(Publisher's Weekly Top Mystery 2016 List)
The Madman's Room (2017)

Other impossible crime novels from Locked Room International:
The Riddle of Monte Verita (Jean-Paul Torok) 2012
The Killing Needle (Henry Cauvin) 2014
The Derek Smith Omnibus (Derek Smith) 2014
(Washington Post Top Fiction Books 2014)
The House That Kills (Noel Vindry) 2015
The Decagon House Murders (Yukito Ayatsuji) 2015
(Publisher's Weekly Top Mystery 2015 List)
Hard Cheese (Ulf Durling) 2015
The Moai Island Puzzle (Alice Arisugawa) 2016
(Washington Post Summer Book List 2016)
The Howling Beast (Noel Vindry) 2016
Death in the Dark (Stacey Bishop) 2017
The Ginza Ghost (Keikichi Osaka) 2017
The Realm of the Impossible (anthology 2017)

Visit our website at www.mylri.com or
www.lockedroominternational.com

DEATH IN THE HOUSE OF RAIN

Szu-Yen Lin

Foreword by Fei Wu

Translated by Szu-Yen Lin

Death in the House of Rain

This book is a work of fiction. The characters, incidents, and dialogue are drawn from the author's imagination and are not to be construed as real. Any resemblance to actual events or persons, living or dead, is entirely coincidental.

To
My parents, for everything

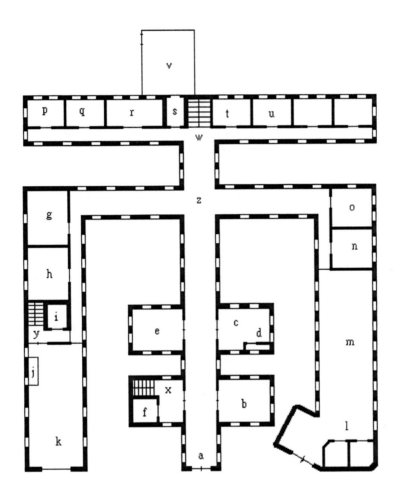

Figure 1. Ground floor of the House of Rain

(a) hallway (b) living room (c) dining room (d) kitchen (e)
recreation room (f) empty room (g) movie room (h) table tennis
room (i) empty room (j) work table (k) garage (l) shower rooms
(m) badminton hall (n) small study (o) piano room (p) Cindy's
room (q) Ru's room (r) servants' living room (s) changing room (t)
laundry (u) stockroom (v) tennis court (w) north staircase (x) south
staircase (y) west staircase (z) intersection of corridors

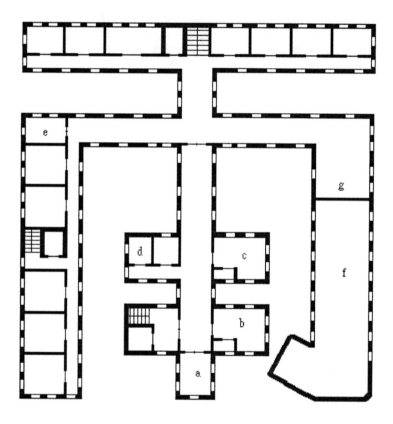

Figure 2. First floor of the House of Rain

(a) study (b) Jingfu Bai's and Yinghan Qiu's room (c) Yuyun Bai's room (d) movie room (e) public shower rooms (f) high ceiling (g) balcony

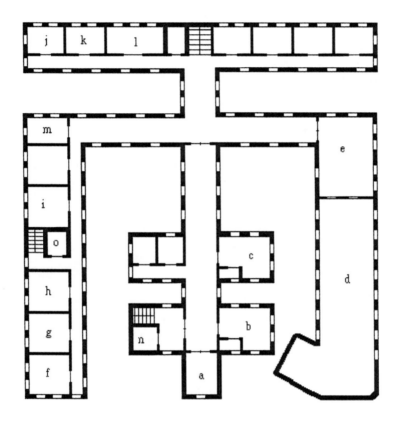

Figure 3. Second floor of the House of Rain

(a) Renze Bai's study (b) Renze Bai's room (c) Lingsha Bai's room
(d) high ceiling (e) library (f) Yunxin Liu's room (g) Xiangya
Yue's room (h) Tingzhi Yan's room (i) guest room (j) Chengyan
Fang's room (k) Bingyu Xu's room (l) Ruoping Lin's room (m)
public shower room (n) empty room (o) empty room

CAST OF CHARACTERS
(names follow western convention)

Past residents of the House of Rain

Jingfu Bai, *renowned entrepreneur, owner of a car company*
Yinghan Qiu, *his wife, housewife*
Yuyun Bai, *their daughter, university student*

Current residents of the House of Rain

Renze Bai, *professor of English, the younger brother of Jingfu Bai*
Lingsha Bai, *his daughter, student in the English department*
Cindy, *maidservant from Indonesia*
Ru, *maidservant*

Lingsha Bai's classmates

Bingyu Xu, a *playboy*
Chengyan Fang, *a persistent young man*
Yunxin Liu, *a young woman with a dominant character*
Xiangya Yue, *a doll-like girl enslaved by Yunxin*
Tingzhi Yan, *a smart and confident young woman*
Zhengyu Jiang, *a silent young man*

Other characters

Shengfeng Shi, *an avant-garde architect*
Wenliu Pan, *his beautiful wife*
Weiqun Yang, *ex-boyfriend of Yinghan Qiu*
Ruoping Lin, *a young assistant professor of philosophy and amateur detective*

CONTENTS

FOREWORD

Fei Wu

Fei Wu is an author, translator, literary agent and publisher, native to China but well-known to, and respected by, western readers. JMP

If you were to ask a western locked room enthusiast to name any Chinese examples of the genre, he or she would in all likelihood mention "The Chinese Gold Murders" (1959), "The Chinese Maze Murders (1962), and *The Red Pavilion* (1964), all featuring Judge Dee, the Tang dynasty magistrate and gifted detective. But no matter how vividly the Dutch author Robert Van Gulik conjured up 7th century China, they remain tales written by a foreigner and cannot be regarded as "pure" Chinese locked room. And, although it is not widely known, China had indeed already produced quite a number of home-grown mysteries prior to Van Gulik.

Mainland China
The origins of Chinese mystery writing can be found in the translations of western works of the genre which poured into the country in the late 19th century as a result of the Second Opium War, when Britain forced China to open itself to imports of all kinds, including literary. Conan Doyle's Sherlock Holmes stories were particularly popular: in 1896, the magazine *The Chinese Progress* published four Holmes cases and by 1916, all four Holmes novels and forty of his short stories had been published in Chinese translations.

In January of 1918, Poe's "The Murders in the Rue Morgue" (1841) was finally published, although its title was changed to the somewhat less catchy "A Miserable Death of Mother and Daughter." By 1919, over four hundred foreign detective novels and short stories had been translated and published in China, including works by R. Austin Freeman, Maurice Leblanc, Baroness Orczy, Fergus Hume, and many more.

In view of such popularity, it was scarcely surprising that local versions of the most famous detectives started to appear. Xiaoqing Cheng's Detective Sang Huo and Liaohong Sun's swashbuckling thief Ping Lu were obviously based on Holmes and Maurice Leblanc's Arsène Lupin respectively; in Cheng's short story "One-sided Love" (1928) the victim was stabbed to death in a locked room. But the honour of being China's very first locked room mystery belonged to "Buddhism Bead" (1923), which appeared in the fourteenth issue of the magazine *Detective World*. It was written by three authors as a chain game and was very creative for the period: the victim lost his head in a locked room.

Other local Chinese publications continued to appear in increasing quality and quantity until the start of hostilities between China and Japan in the 1930s. For the next forty years, the Second World War, the rise of Chinese communism, and Mao's Cultural Revolution effectively stifled the progress of literary development, and controls were not eased until the milestone year of 1979, which saw the publication of Agatha Christie's *Death on the Nile* in *Translations* magazine and Ellery Queen's *The Greek Coffin Mystery* by QunZhong Press.

Nevertheless, it was not until 2000 or thereabouts that the really rapid development of China's own native mysteries, including locked room, occurred. The principal driving force was the internet, where many mystery websites, blogs and forums started to appear, sharing information on the subject, the foremost being *tuili.com*. One of its features was to allow subscribers to share their own stories. It wasn't long before high-quality locked room mysteries started to appear. In 2001, a short story entitled "Murder in a Moving Locked Room" was posted, wherein the victim was found dismembered in the rear compartment of a truck which had never left the sight of the following police car from the moment the victim entered it to the time the police opened it. The trick was original and ingenious and the story can be seen as the pioneer of modern China locked room mysteries.

Starting in 2007, Chinese publishers started to climb on the band-wagon, publishing the works of John Dickson Carr and Japanese *honkaku* (Golden Age fair-play style) writers, such as Shimada Soji, Maya Yutaka, Mitsuda Shinzo, Arisugawa Arisu, and Nikaido Reito. Full disclosure: my jointly-owned company, Murder Pen, has published over forty such books since being founded in 2010, introducing readers to Clayton Rawson, Hake Talbot, Christianna Brand, Paul Halter, and many more.

Meanwhile, in January of 2006, the magazine *Tuili* had been launched in Beijing ("Tuili" is Chinese pinyin for "mystery"). It was the first local magazine almost exclusively dedicated to the works of Chinese authors, and provided the opportunity for writers previously dabbling on internet sites to be taken seriously. The very first issue of *Tuili* featured an excellent impossible-crime story: "34 New Leather Shoes," a classic no-footprints-in-the-snow puzzle.

Due to the fact that *Tuili* only publishes short stories, aspiring authors, for whom the magazine offers the best chance of recognition, tend to use this format. It is for this reason that most Chinese locked rooms are of short story length. Their biggest strength is the jaw-dropping mysteries themselves, which are often audaciously creative. Examples are: a dismembered body on virgin snow ("Sacrifice in the Snow"); a perfect locked room consisting of a concrete cube ("The Rules of Sin"); teleported locked rooms ("The Magic of Teleport", "The Ultimate Magic of Teleport"). Each of these stories is a minor masterpiece.

On the other hand, some authors expend too much energy on the trick at the expense of the pace of the story and development of the characters. In an over-written tape locked room story ("Hell of Tape"), the author reveals solutions to 20 tape tricks! Another weakness is the use of narrative tricks to deceive the reader (for example, when the narrator turns out to be a fly). Such tricks are seldom appreciated. To be fair, most of the authors are young, with a tendency to exuberance, which can sometimes lead to a lack of sober judgment.

Taiwan

The history of the publication of foreign-language mysteries was very different in Taiwan, which had been ceded to Japan from 1895 to 1945. It was not until 1950 that the full collection of Holmes stories was published, and even then it was as a series of children's books! Regardless of the late start, Taiwan had caught up and was even beginning to surpass the mainland very soon afterwards. In 1969, Foer Lin founded Lin Bai Publishing Ltd., a publishing house focusing on the translation of Japan mysteries. Its books dominated the market in the 1960s and 1970s, during which time very few mysteries from the UK or US were published. In 1984, he founded *Mystery Magazine* which continued his propensity to feature Japanese mysteries to the detriment of US, European, or local Taiwanese stories.

The situation changed in 1994, when Rye Field Publishing Co. introduced S.S. Van Dine, Lawrence Block, Patricia Cornwell, and Minette Walters to Taiwanese readers. Since then, many more UK and US mysteries have become available. In 1997, Hung-Tze Jan (one of the three judges of the *Shimada Soji Mystery Award*, see below) set up Murder Shop, which has remained the biggest mystery publication project in the Taiwanese market ever since. He selected one hundred and one classic UK/US and European books—a large number at the time—not only Golden Age, but hard boiled, spy, suspense etc., covering every category of mystery.

Another big year for foreign mystery publication in Taiwan was 2004. Faces Publishing Ltd. introduced the works of John Dickson Carr to Taiwanese fans, and Crown Publishing Ltd. republished Shimada Soji's *The Tokyo Zodiac Murders*, which it had previously published in 1988. Since then, many more contemporary Japanese authors and Golden Age English-language writers have become available. The rights to foreign works seem easier to acquire than in China.

Another factor contributing to the continuing growth in the Taiwanese market is the various awards founded after 2000. Notably, in 2003, the *Werewolf Castle Mystery Literature Award*, later to become the *Mystery Writers of Taiwan (MWT) Award*, was founded; and in 2009, the *Shimada Soji Mystery Award* was established, the latter being open to Chinese-language writers from all over the world, providing a strong incentive to young writers. (In China, on the other hand, awards have not flourished: even one founded by *Tuili* magazine foundered after three years.)

Conclusion

Due to the many factors explained above, the number of authors capable of writing top quality impossible crime stories is growing fast. Some of the shining names are Qing Ji and Szu-Yen Lin from Taiwan, and Qinwen Sun, Junfei Sun, Zhuan Du and many more from China mainland. Qinwen Sun has a remarkable record: since 2008, he has written almost forty locked room short stories. Junfei Sun is known for his imaginative puzzles, which rival those of Shimada Soji.

In contrast, according to a recent survey, there have been only fifteen locked room novels in mainland China and seven in Taiwan since 2004, showing the extreme preponderance of the short version.

To sum up, authors from China and Taiwan have already produced many excellent locked room mysteries, but there is still room for improvement, particularly in novel-length stories.

Fei Wu
Shanghai
2017

PROLOGUE:
DARKNESS IN THE RAIN

A rainy night.

A small sedan wound its lonely way along the circuitous mountain road, carrying a silent couple.

The man, who was driving, gazed at the winding road.

The woman beside him looked tired.

'Can't we do this another day?' she asked in a feeble voice.

'Lingsha wants it today. It's not a detour, since we'd have passed by the House of Rain anyway.'

'You spoil her,' sighed the woman.

'Why not take a nap? You must be tired.'

The woman knew it was useless to argue. She sighed again and closed her eyes.

Night fell and darkness permeated the chilly air. The lightless road loomed ominously like a black snake. Raindrops fell like tears from the weeping sky.

Driving in such weather was suicide, but the man didn't seem to care much.

The road ahead forked like the tongue of a poisonous snake. The sedan turned left and crawled onto a narrow path. The woman was already nodding with fatigue.

The path circled the mountainside and led to an opening in a forest. The silhouette of a huge building with scattered lights appeared ahead.

The incessant raindrops hit the top of the sedan like drumbeats.

The man pulled on the handbrake. The woman opened her eyes.

As he was about to turn off the engine, a figure appeared in the sedan's headlights. The woman gasped.

The figure froze, staring at them. It turned suddenly and disappeared into the darkness.

It was a man with a crew cut, looking frightened, his right arm swathed in bandages. He was wearing blue jeans and a jacket. They caught a glimpse of a square face with thick eyebrows.

Shortly thereafter the couple heard a car engine start nearby. Presently an automobile went past and vanished into the darkness.

'Who…who was that?' said the woman, startled.

The man stroked his stubbled chin and frowned. 'I met him once before. He's Yinghan's friend.'

'Why did he look so frightened?'

'Who knows? Let's go inside and find out. Yuyun should be home.' The man pocketed the key and got out.

'It's raining!'

The woman was still taking an umbrella out from under her seat by the time the man reached the house.

It was a three-story building, a huge monster under the night sky.

The man went up the front steps and tried the double-doors of the hallway. They were not locked.

He pushed it open and stepped inside.

The light in the hallway was on, dim and dingy, creating a mysterious atmosphere. He moved forward, leaving wet footprints on the floor. There was a large living room to the right; a set of double-doors open to the left revealed a staircase leading upwards.

'You should dry your shoes first!'

The woman's voice came from behind. She was drying her shoes at the front door.

The man looked at the staircase. There were dirty, hasty footprints going upstairs.

He spoke to the woman thoughtfully:

'Things aren't right. Are their bedrooms on the first floor?'

'Yes. But—'

The man didn't wait for the woman to finish. He turned on the light and went up the stairs.

More dingy lighting.

There was another set of double-doors at the first floor landing. The dirty footprints continued through the open doors to a dark corridor, beyond which he could see light streaming weakly from a half-open door.

As the man was about to walk through the double-doors, he noticed something lying on the floor to his right.

There was a small room right beside the stairway; the thing lay in front of the room, the door of which was closed.

The man stood frozen, his mouth open.

It was a girl with long hair, her limbs spread apart, her eyes wide open, and her tongue protruding from her mouth. Her red long-sleeved shirt had been pushed upwards to reveal white underwear and uncovered breasts. Her black slacks and underpants had been discarded beside her.

There was a line—probably a fishing line—around the poor girl's neck.

'Where are they?' The woman's voice came from below.

'Don't—.'

It was too late. The woman screamed and drew back at the sight of the body, almost losing her balance. 'What…what's that?'

'Call the police!'

'Is that….'

'Hurry up!'

The woman stumbled back and fumbled for her cell phone.

After briefly examining the girl's body, the man walked through the double-doors and into the corridor. He pushed open the half-closed door.

The light inside was weak. The room was magnificently furnished, but....

There was a queen-sized bed opposite the door. On it lay a naked woman with her face twisted and her eyes open wide.

On the floor lay a man in trousers and a coat. The soles of his leather shoes were stained with dirt, which explained the footprints in the house. His face was a red mess, brains and blood spread around.

A blood-stained hatchet lay beside the body.

Backing out of the room, the man fought back the urge to vomit.

'Are they all right?' The woman's trembling voice came from the staircase.

The man turned and answered in a hoarse voice.

'They're all dead.'

PART ONE:
CONCERTO IN THE RAIN

Chapter 1 Drifting Souls

1 *(February 10, 3.40 p.m.)*

The Southern Cross-Island Highway was bathed in heavy rain. Coldness permeated the air.

Ruoping turned the wheel cautiously. He had been driving for a while after passing the Heaven Lake, where there was a temple in honour of the workers killed during the construction of the highway.

'Turn left when you see a red road sign. Drive along the path and you'll see the House of Rain.'

Bearing the guide in mind, Ruoping slowed the car. As soon as he passed a road sign that read "FALLING ROCKS," there was a huge sound from behind and the road shuddered simultaneously. He stopped the car, turned round in the seat and looked through the back window.

There was no doubt, it was a landslide and the road was now completely blocked by falling rocks, from which protruded the half-buried road sign.

Ruoping, realising he'd better get out of there as quickly as possible, stepped on the accelerator.

After several turns on the road a red sign appeared on the left. The words on it were barely discernible.

'At last.' Ruoping heaved a sigh of relief.

He made a left turn onto a path in the woods and slowed down.

There was a dark moment before the view suddenly broadened. He was stunned by what he saw.

A huge grey building stood ahead like a silent beast in the rain. On the leftmost part of the building was an iron door, separated from the front door—a set of double-doors—by an open space. There was another set of double-doors on the rightmost side, facing south-west.

This was the House of Rain, a three-dimensional presentation of the Chinese character for "rain," as seen from a bird's-eye view, which meant that, when he was facing the front door, Ruoping was visually at the base of the character.

Why anyone would construct such a curious edifice in such a remote spot was utterly beyond him. The previous owner had been Jingfu Bai, a renowned entrepreneur. He had built this house as a retirement home for his handicapped father—or for himself, as some people suspected. His father had died shortly after the family moved in. The current residents were Jingfu Bai's younger brother, his brother's daughter, and two maidservants.

As Ruoping was looking for a place to park, the iron door on the left started to roll up, and at the same time the front door opened to reveal a middle-aged man nodding to him and pointing to the iron door.

Ruoping manoeuvred his black Ford into the opening revealed, which turned out to be a spacious garage capable of accommodating nine vehicles in three rows. There were two cars inside already, a Mercedes-Benz and a Yulon. Ruoping parked in the leftmost space of the second row, got out and surveyed the garage.

Yellow streams of light came from the ceiling, mixing with the natural light from the windows. On the other side of the garage were two doors: a set of double-doors to the left, and a small red door to the right, on which a calendar was hanging. Between the double-doors and the wall to the left stood a work table, on the top of which lay a variety of tools.

The small red door opened. The man Ruoping had just seen appeared.

'Nice to meet you. I am Renze Bai.' He held out his hand with a friendly smile and shook Ruoping's hand firmly.

Bai's facial features were finely chiselled and his hair was combed back sleekly. He gave the impression of being well-cultivated.

Bai taught English literature at a university in Tainan. He had completed his doctoral degree in the United States and had rapidly become a renowned literary critic after returning to Taiwan. Ruoping had attended one of his lectures and been impressed by his erudition. Aside from being an academic, Bai was also an intellectual who had written a lot on public matters.

'Thank you for coming,' he said. 'The weather is so unpredictable. I hope I didn't cause you any inconvenience.'

'Not at all. And I've never had the opportunity to witness a landslide before today. It's quite an experience.'

'A landslide?'

'Yes. On my way here. A lucky escape.' Ruoping briefly explained what had happened.

'Oh dear, I'm so sorry. I'll do my best to compensate during your stay. Now, let me show you around. This way, please.'

Ruoping followed the professor through the red door and into a corridor.

There were three large rooms on the left, facing several windows on the right. The window curtains were open, but the lights along the corridor were off, probably because it was still afternoon. The rain hit the windows and made them blurry.

'This is the table tennis room, and that is the movie room.' Bai pointed at the last two rooms in the corridor. 'Feel free to use them. I expect you will be staying for a couple of days.'

'Thanks. By the way, do we have any other guests today?'

'Yes. I expect you noticed the third car in the garage?' The professor turned right at the end of the corridor and another corridor extended before them. 'That Yulon belongs to one of my daughter's friends. She invited a couple of them over and they will be staying for a few days. Will that affect your investigation?'

'No. It's perfectly okay.'

'Good.' Bai stopped at the crossing of two corridors. 'Let me familiarize you with the environment. If you turn left here you'll reach the servants' rooms, laundry, and the north stairway. If you keep going you'll see the piano room and the back door to the badminton hall. If you turn right, the corridor will lead you to the dining room, the recreation room, the living room and the front door of the house. Lingsha's friends are all in the living room. Let's go and greet them.'

They turned right. Sets of open double-doors could be seen to the left and to the right. Ruoping could see that the room on the right was the recreation room, containing a billiards table and a card table. The room on the left was the dining room, in the centre of which stood a huge dining table, with a small kitchen in the corner.

Since the house was a physical presentation of the Chinese character "rain," there should be two more rooms ahead, for the character in question has four dots in its lower middle part.

'I forgot to mention it,' the professor turned and whispered to Ruoping, 'but I've told them you're here for academic purposes.

There's no need to let them know everything. I didn't even tell Lingsha.'

'Good idea.'

'We'll get down to business after dinner.'

'I'm fine with any arrangement.'

Bai pointed to the next room on the left. 'This is the living room.'

The double-doors of the living room were open, facing another set of double-doors across the corridor. Directly before them at the end of the corridor was the front door of the house, with a shoe rack standing beside it.

The bleakness of the house kept reminding Ruoping of the terrifying scene of falling rocks, resulting in a pervasive uneasiness in his mind.

As they entered the living room, Ruoping heard a man shouting and a woman screaming, which invoked in him a strong premonition of imminent tragedy.

2 *(February 10, 4.00 p.m.)*

'Are you sure this house isn't haunted, Lingsha?'

It was Bingyu Xu, a young man with gelled and dyed blonde hair, who was asking the question, arms folded across his chest and an unlit cigarette between his lips.

'You asked the same question just a few moments ago,' replied Lingsha.

'Stop asking stupid questions. It's rude,' said Chengyan Fang impatiently, waving his hand at Bingyu.

It was four o'clock in the afternoon and the rain was still falling heavily outside. Lingsha surveyed her classmates in the living room. The dismal atmosphere made them look like prisoners. On the table were cups holding brown liquid—coffee.

'All right, I won't ask again,' said Bingyu, flicking the cigarette with his fingers.

'I appreciate your cooperation,' said the girl.

Bingyu Xu was a notorious playboy. All his time was spent on dressing up and dating. He'd recently dumped a girl who was intensely infatuated with him, which had made his reputation even worse.

'This rain…it's getting heavier,' said Chengyan before taking a sip of his coffee.

'The heaviest I've ever seen. But we're safe inside,' said Lingsha.

'We should always treat weather forecasts as ironic,' joked Chengyan, but no one appreciated his attempt at humour.

Chengyan Fang was a handsome young man. Lingsha had previously thought of him as having a persistent nature, but this time he gave up on his joke and sank into the sofa with unfocused eyes.

'Where are the princess and her maidservant?' Bingyu threw the unlit cigarette into the ashtray, and took out a new one.

'I've no idea.' Chengyan shook his head.

'Lingsha?' She shook her head, too.

'Hey, why did you ask about your Princess Yunxin?' asked Chengyan suddenly, putting down his cup.

'Just mind your Princess Xiangya,' retorted the playboy.

Chengyan drew himself up straight in the sofa, staring at Bingyu and clenching his fists.

'Stop!' said Lingsha in a loud voice.

Why did men always act like this? Although they never came to blows, it was still unsettling to watch them crossing verbal swords.

'Sorry.' Bingyu smiled at Lingsha, lit a cigarette, and flamboyantly puffed a few smoke rings.

'I don't want to have to remind you that it's smoke-free in here.' The rainstorm was still raging outside and these two men were distracting her.

As the playboy reluctantly stubbed his cigarette in the ash tray, footsteps could be heard in the corridor. Bingyu tilted his head and smiled disdainfully towards the entrance of the living room.

A tall, slender figure appeared. Yunxin Liu wore a red sweater and a black skirt; a silver moon-shaped necklace hung from her neck. Everything about her suggested indifference, arrogance and dominance. She wasn't particularly beautiful but, with her short hair and cold eyes, she exuded a strange magnetism.

Lingsha didn't like Yunxin. She seemed affected, overbearing and selfish.

'So you're all here. Xiangya and I were sorting out the luggage.'

As if walking on an imaginary catwalk, Yunxin stepped into the living room. Her red toenails were in strong contrast with the black sandals making loud sounds on the floor.

What a dramatic entrance, thought Lingsha.

A petite figure revealed itself behind Yunxin. It was Xiangya Yue.

Lingsha felt sympathy for the girl. Xiangya's delicate facial features made her look like a doll in a showcase. She wore her hair in a ponytail and was wearing a smart dress. She appeared timid and avoided eye contact with everyone, making a point of sitting down after Yunxin.

'Which floor is your room on?' asked Bingyu with a smile.

'The second. The same as yours,' said Yunxin coldly, eyeing Chengyan instead.

Chengyan shuffled uneasily and squinted at Xiangya.

The doll lowered her head, her eyes expressionless.

'I want some coffee,' announced Yunxin, frowning at the plates and cups on the table. 'Xiangya, get me some.'

'Where do I get it?' Xiangya's voice was feeble and her manner obsequious.

'Work it out for yourself!'

'I'll get you some.' Lingsha stood up, finding her legs stiff. 'Keep your shirt on,' she said coldly.

Yunxin met her gaze with the same coldness:

'As you wish, Princess Lingsha.'

Lingsha left without answering.

Cindy was in the kitchen. She was a young woman with dark skin, curly hair and bright eyes.

'Could you make two more cups of coffee for me? I'll take them to the living room myself,' said Lingsha.

The maidservant nodded and set to work right away.

Cindy was from Indonesia. She worked hard and never complained. She was the opposite of Xiangya. Cindy would sing Indonesian songs when cooking, while Xiangya always appeared absent-minded when serving Yunxin.

Holding the tray, Lingsha walked back to the living room. She couldn't understand why that adorable girl would subject herself to that dominant princess. It was a mystery.

In the living room, Yunxin was sitting with her arms crossed over her chest and her head tilted. Chengyan was sitting opposite her with his head tilted as well. Xiangya, not knowing what to do, shifted her gaze from one to the other. Bingyu was smilingly puffing smoke rings which irritated everyone.

How had things ended up like this? Lingsha had never intended any of it to happen. At first she'd only invited Xiangya, but then....

Lingsha put the tray down in front of Yunxin and sat down on the sofa. The other picked up a cup and saucer and quickly took a sip without saying anything.

'Ah!' The cup and saucer dropped to the floor and broke.

'So hot!' Yunxin neatly avoided the splashing liquid, but banged her knee against the table. Chengyan started to laugh, but her stony glare stopped him.

From the corridor came sounds of other people talking. Lingsha recognised her father's voice.

'Laugh all you want,' said Yunxin, getting up. 'I know you hate the sight of me. Good. Let's settle this today.'

Chengyan's expression changed and he, too, stood up.

Lingsha noticed they were about the same height, roughly five feet seven.

'Hell's Bells! You're not even worth my attention,' announced Chengyan, giving Yunxin an icy look.

Lingsha had never seen him like this, and suddenly realised how little she knew about her classmates....

'You...,' Yunxin's face was red with anger.

Chengyan remained unmoved as he replied: 'You've enslaved Xiangya because you envy her beauty and talent. Your arrogance only betrays your sense of inferiority.'

'Enough!' shouted Bingyu as Yunxin started to scream. Chengyan, who seemed to be startled by the sudden outburst, stared at him. Xiangya looked at them fearfully and helplessly.

As Lingsha was getting ready to calm her furious guests down, there was an interruption.

'Ladies and gentlemen, may I introduce...What's going on?'

Upon hearing the familiar voice, Lingsha breathed a sigh of relief and sank back in the sofa.

3 (February 10, 4.20 p.m.)

As Ruoping entered the living room with the professor, he saw five young people inside.

Two of them were standing: a tall young woman in red with short hair and a good-looking young man with sharp facial features and bushy eyebrows. The former was eying the latter like a hungry tigress, while he in turn was looking coldly at another young man who was smoking.

Aside from the woman in red and the good-looking man, the man smoking also looked indignant, his sharp eyes half covered by his dyed blonde hair. The cigarette between his lips was creating an uncomfortable fug in the room.

Two people were sitting on the sofa: a young woman with white skin and long hair and a second young woman with fine exquisite features and pale skin.

'What's going on in here?' asked Bai in a reproachful tone. 'Smoking is not allowed!'

'Sorry,' said the three angry people in chorus before they turned in different directions. Two of them sat down abruptly. The third stubbed his cigarette out reluctantly.

'Don't worry, Dad.' The woman with long hair stood up and gave Bai a reassuring smile. 'It's not important. Come and sit down.' She acknowledged Ruoping's presence with a nod. Ruoping nodded back.

'Allow me to introduce this gentleman,' said the professor, clearing his throat. 'Mr. Ruoping Lin took my courses when he was an undergraduate. He currently teaches philosophy at Tianhe University and is here to discuss a paper on literary values with me. He's my honoured guest and will be staying for a couple of days.'

Ruoping didn't know how many of them were listening. Nobody was looking at him.

'Have a seat, Ruoping. I'll get you a cup of coffee.' The professor patted Ruoping on the shoulder and said to Lingsha: 'Introduce your friends to Mr. Lin.'

After Bai left, Ruoping settled down in a chair next to Lingsha, who soon began a brief introduction.

'The cool guy with the blonde hair is Bingyu Xu. He's a ladies' man, very good at blowing smoke rings. He'll show you if you ask him. The man beside Bingyu is Chengyan Fang, who drove everyone here. He's quite a romantic person....'

The two young men's anger evaporated before Lingsha's compliments.

'The fashionable lady is Yunxin Liu. People call her the Queen of Fashion. The other lady is Xiangya Yue, who's a wonderful pianist....' Lingsha paused. 'Oh, and I almost forgot: there's another lady called Tingzhi Yan, but she's in her room because of a slight illness. They're all my classmates. We're all seniors in the English literature department.'

As Lingsha's introduction came to an end, Bai returned with a cup of coffee on a saucer.

'Thank you so much,' said Ruoping.

'My pleasure,' Bai smiled. 'Dinner will be at six o'clock sharp. The dining room is just next door. I have to go now. Make yourself at home...Lingsha, show Mr. Lin to his room.'

The moment the professor left, Bingyu stood up with a scowl on his face. He put his hands in the pockets of his jeans and left.

Yunxin stared coldly at his receding back then she, too, stood up and left. Xiangya Yue followed her out like a frightened rabbit. Chengyan Fang was the last to leave.

Ruoping took a sip of his coffee and looked at the window. The design on the pink curtains distracted his attention from the rain outside. There were six windows in the living room, all with the same curtain design.

'Was it you who invited them over?' asked Ruoping.

Lingsha paused before answering. 'At first I only invited Xiangya, but somehow everyone came along with her. I don't really mind having more guests since this is a big house.'

'So Xiangya Yue is your good friend.'

'She helped me with the final exam of the music course. To thank her I suggested she spend a few days of the winter vacation here.'

Lingsha's manner was refined, probably influenced by her father's background. But she didn't seem pedantic. On the contrary, her face, framed by long, soft hair, showed quiet determination.

'You're not very close to the other classmates, are you?' asked Ruoping.

Lingsha hesitated for a moment. 'No. But I knew they'd been wanting to visit this house.'

'Do you know why they were so keen?'

'I don't know and I don't want to know,' said Lingsha gloomily.

She was probably still haunted by what happened here last year, thought Ruoping. It was impossible to erase such trauma from one's memory....

'By the way, where do those double-doors opposite lead?' Ruoping had been wanting to ask since he first saw them.

'To the staircase. No one goes up that way anymore because of...what happened. That part of the first floor has been abandoned since then. Actually, the two entrances into that area haven't been locked until this gathering.'

'Which two entrances?'

'The set of double-doors in the south staircase and another set at the intersection of corridors.'

'Did the maidservants ever clean the area before it was locked?'

'No. The rooms in that area are no longer in use. Dad said there was no need to do any cleaning.'

'I see.'

Ruoping's cup was already empty. It was still raining cats and dogs outside. The beating of the raindrops on the windows sounded hollow. The air inside was stifling.

The events which had taken three lives last year had occurred in that forbidden area, which had now been abandoned for almost a year, like a heavy stone buried deep in the sea. He felt a chill run down his spine.

While both of them were lost in thought, some strange sounds—presumably footsteps—came from the ceiling above, or, more precisely, the floor of that accursed area.

The chill spread through him. Ruoping gave Lingsha a quick glance. She was still lost in thought and didn't appear to have noticed.

'There were footsteps coming from upstairs.' Ruoping broke the silence. 'Did you hear them?'

The girl looked up with a sudden jerk, as if struck by lightning. She gazed at Ruoping with surprise and terror in her eyes.

4 *(February 10, 4.40 p.m.)*

'That nitwit!'

Chengyan Fang leant against the door.

He was in his room. His baggage lay scattered on the tidy bed.

The room was in the northwest corner of the second floor. There was one window on the western wall and two on the northern one, curtains all drawn now. Beside the door there was a bathroom. Lingsha had told them that each room had a bathroom and a double bed. The house was like a hotel.

The light was dim. Actually most lights here were dim. This might be due to the eccentric taste of the previous owner of the house. It didn't bother him.

So he was finally here, but things weren't going well.

He'd decided to come along when Xiangya had said she'd been invited. It would have seemed odd if he'd come alone. He'd told Bingyu Xu about the invitation and the latter had suggested they go together. And it was no surprise that Yunxin Liu would come with her maidservant.

He'd been crazy about Xiangya, but had never succeeded in asking her out. Now he finally had a chance to be with her in the same place. He had to seize his chance....

Some of his classmates had given up the thought of visiting the house because of the tragedy the previous year. They even suspected that Lingsha's mind might have suffered after that tragic event. Not even Lingsha's closest friends had ever set foot in the place. Fortunately, she was mature enough to cope with everything.

But none of these mattered as long as no one interfered with his plan. A friend had warned him against coming to this so-called haunted house, but he hadn't taken any notice. The guy was obsessed with the paranormal and horror movies. No need to take what he'd said seriously.

Chengyan went into the bathroom and washed his face. It made him feel refreshed. He went back to the bed and sat down.

Bingyu was such a nuisance. Everyone could see that he'd come here with a purpose: Yunxin Liu. He'd slept with every girl he'd dated. He was a scum because he didn't know what love was. Love isn't sex, and sex should be dedicated to first love.

Chengyan unzipped the backpack lying on the bed, took out a notebook and opened it with care.

There was a photo glued to the first page: Xiangya and he were standing together in a pavilion with the sea behind them. She was in sportswear and gym shoes. Her smile was charming and very appealing.

It was the only photo of him with Xiangya, taken two years ago, when they and others had visited Kenting National Park. It served well as the first page of the notebook.

Taking a deep breath, he turned the subsequent pages slowly and carefully.

They all contained photos of Xiangya: Xiangya in class, on campus, smiling, chatting, absent-minded....

Some of the photos were from the online albums of Xiangya's friends; some were his own efforts, starting from the first day they'd met. It hadn't always been easy to take them without being caught, but, so far, his luck had held.

To him, Xiangya was like a doll that had come alive from a fairy tale, dreamy and unreal. She was the creation of an inspired artist. The dainty figurine was unlike anything else you could expect to find in the mundane world.

He remembered reading a short story, "Love Story before Dawn," written by the Taiwanese writer Nao Weng during the Japanese rule. The story was about a young man yearning for love, which was a perfect portrayal of his situation.

He had been waiting for the right time. He would free her from Yunxin Liu. Xiangya would appreciate his help. It was time to take action....

Speaking of Yunxin... he wondered why Xiangya had suddenly become her slave three months ago. There was something fishy about that, but so far he hadn't found any clues.

He must save her. It was a pain to see her suffer. He would have hit Yunxin if Bingyu hadn't been there in the living room with them. He couldn't stand her arrogance any more.

Chengyan closed the notebook and put it away. He lay down on the bed.

Bingyu made him upset. The guy was more like a business partner than a friend, which might very well be how Bingyu thought about him. But he had to be careful to avoid any conflict with him, so as to make sure nothing would stand in his way.

Looking up at the ceiling, he felt tired. He'd driven everyone here from the city centre and hadn't had any time to rest.

An hour and a quarter to go before dinner. He should go over his plan as soon as possible.

He got up and walked to the window. It was hazy outside. He remembered that the professor had promised to give him a DVD as a present after dinner.

A thriller. He liked the genre very much, especially when the thrills were combined with love stories. In that particular film, a young man fell in love with a girl, but was unable to win her heart. At some point the two of them went with other friends to explore a cave and stayed there overnight. The young man sealed the entrance to the cave so that he could stay longer with the girl. The others fought him after they found what he'd done. The young man did away with all of them, but was eventually put to death by the girl he loved. He'd been fascinated by the eerie feeling of the film and its atmosphere of gloom and doom... After seeing it in the movie theatre, he'd been waiting for the DVD release. It just so happened that Bai had the DVD and was happy to give it away.

He looked vacantly at the mist outside.

Confining the one you love and yourself to a closed space... how romantic and desperate.

He turned to his backpack and took out a small glass bottle full of pills. A half-smile appeared on his face.

5 *(February 10, 6.00 p.m.)*

Dinner started at six o'clock.

In addition to Cindy, there was a second maidservant serving dinner. Her name was Ru. She was probably under twenty and was tall and neat with a round face. Lingsha had said that Ru was the daughter of a close friend, and had volunteered to work there to support her family, starting that winter.

A young woman in a ponytail appeared at the door of the dining room. Though not particularly beautiful, she exuded an intellectual glamour. She was like a mix of Lingsha Bai and Yunxin Liu, a perfect blend of softness and toughness, of coldness and warmth. She was wearing jeans and a black jacket and her steps were firm and determined.

'Tingzhi.' Lingsha waved her hand. 'Are you feeling better? Take a seat.'

'Thanks. I'm feeling better,' Tingzhi Yan replied with a smile that inspired confidence.

Lingsha introduced her to Ruoping, who was impressed by her self-assured manner. Shortly afterwards, dinner came to an end.

Ruoping had made an appointment with the professor for nine o'clock, but it was still early, so he decided to explore the mansion further.

Stepping out of the dining room, he turned right and went to where the corridors intersected. He turned right again. Now he was in the eastern wing of the house. The inevitable dim lights along the corridor created a sense of eerie serenity.

In the wall to his left were four windows with beautiful curtains. Through the windows he could only see darkness, but he could tell it was still pouring with rain. The atmosphere was ominous, and the guests there only made the feeling stronger.

Bingyu Xu—frivolous; Chengyan Fang—persistent; Yunxin Liu—arrogant; Xiangya Yue—obedient; Tingzhi Yan—confident. It was curious that these particular people would have come here together. They didn't seem to be good friends at all and there were obvious conflicts between them.

Another thing troubling him was the footsteps from the first floor.

What Lingsha had said at the time came to mind:

'Footsteps? Are you sure? No one is likely to be up there.' She'd smiled weakly. 'You can't hear clearly with the heavy rain pouring down outside. Don't try to scare me.'

'Sorry. It must have been something else.'

It could have been, but he didn't think so.

But he was too tired to work out the answer and decided to put it aside for the time being.

Ruoping kept walking along the corridor until he was facing a door, which he remembered was the piano room.

He turned right and walked towards the end of the corridor, where the door opening on to the badminton hall faced him. He opened it.

It was dark inside. He fumbled around on the wall and finally found the light switch. Ruoping looked up and saw that the hall was three floors high. There were lights on both the eastern and western walls.

There were four courts in a row with the nets up. He walked across the courts and reached two rooms against the south wall used for showering and changing. The exit from the hall was to the right of the shower room. That would be the double-doors he'd seen from the outside when he arrived.

Ruoping turned and looked back. There was a small balcony up on the first floor for spectators.

His first thought was of someone falling from it, but he tried to put it out of his mind.

I'd better stop thinking about murder and death wherever I go, he told himself.

Ruoping turned off the lights, leaving the ominous balcony in darkness.

6 (Zhengyu Jiang's Soliloquy)

Ten o'clock at night.

I'm in my room, sitting on the bed, my chin resting on my hand.

It's dark inside.

The rainstorm is getting stronger and it is getting colder inside. It would be great to have a good sleep in this kind of weather but I don't feel like it now.

This is the time you can lose yourself in thought, thinking about yourself, the past, the present and the future.

I'm an onlooker.

Yes, an onlooker, outside of the world. There's always an invisible wall separating me from others. I am not part of this world.

The only way to avoid harm and hence be happy is to keep oneself isolated from everything. I had suffered too much before discovering this wisdom.

I began building a high wall around myself and left only one window in it, through which I could observe the world in a detached manner.

When one remains distant from everything, one has the chance to appreciate beauty more. I've been a connoisseur of young women, two of which I consider to be great "artworks"....

Tingzhi Yan and Xiangya Yue.

Tingzhi is more than her looks. Much of her appeal comes from her confidence, brightness, independence and poise. She seems like the sort of detective that could solve a cold case on her own.

Whenever Tingzhi was consuming my thoughts, I would try to shift my attention to Xiangya.

Xiangya's appearance is almost too perfect to be true, like a doll which has come to life. She should be in the showcase of a department store.

But Xiangya, like every doll, lacks a soul, which Tingzhi has. I can see life in Tingzhi's eyes. She is determined and independent, a captivating mixture of intellect, maturity, and independence. But Xiangya is just a beautiful hollow statue, an item in a collection.

Tingzhi is my purpose in being here.

I open my eyes.

The soap opera in the living room before dinner had upset me. Bingyu was a fool. All he did was act cool in front of Yunxin, even if he knew he had no chance of winning her heart.

As for Chengyan, everyone can see that he's infatuated with Xiangya. Although he's tried to conceal his feelings, I'm sure they can be read in his eyes. He seems to be the kind of person that would do crazy things for love.

I believe that in the end Chengyan will realise that Xiangya is just a dream, a dream that will come to an end one day.

One thing I'd never thought I'd enjoy was the manner in which Xiangya succumbed to Yunxin. Some artworks appear more beautiful when destroyed. Xiangya is no doubt that kind of art.

My thoughts shift to Ruoping Lin. I hadn't expected the man's presence. But it seems he's only here to do some research, so there's no need to worry.

I've been observing these miserable people with complete detachment. I am an onlooker, just as I have always been. I'm invisible and omniscient; no one will and no one can notice my presence. I have God's eyes here in this house....

I get off the bed and stretch myself. It's stuffy, but I can't open the window because it's raining.

I decide to leave the room and get some fresh air.

I open the door. There is a deathly silence in the corridor.

While I'm wandering around, a loud thud out of nowhere breaks the silence. It sounds like an object hitting the floor.

The sound came from downstairs. What is it?

I walk uneasily to the staircase and quietly descend the stairs.

As soon as I reach the bottom of the stairs I freeze.

I see it.

There is something with a small tail lying on the floor some distance away.

I venture two steps forward and try hard to identify what it is....

As it dawns on me what I am looking at, I jerk back convulsively.

I gasp and almost faint.

It's the head of a girl.

7 *(February 10, 8.30 pm.)*

Ruoping's room was on the north side of the second floor, one of the most spacious guest rooms in the house. Bai had arranged the room for him because he was a special visitor. However, the spaciousness resulted in hollowness.

Ruoping lay on the bed, which was so soft that he started feeling sleepy. Everything around him began swirling....

Darkness fell.

When he opened his eyes again, it was already eight-thirty. He got off the bed, grabbed his toiletries and clothes from the backpack, and rushed to the bathroom.

He left his room at five minutes to nine. A figure was moving in the corridor.

It was Chengyan Fang, who nodded at him.

'Hi,' said Ruoping, 'is your room on this floor?'

The other nodded. 'Where are you going?'

'I'm going to meet the professor.'

'Really? Me too. He promised to give me a DVD.' Chengyan's face appeared gloomy under the dim light.

'I see. Let's go together.'

At the head of the north staircase they turned right, heading southwards.

'What DVD?' asked Ruoping.

'*Cave of Death.*'

'A box office success, as I recall.'

'Yeah.'

'You like thrillers?'

'Yeah.'

Ruoping pushed open the double-doors in front of them and continued along the corridor. They passed two doors to their left and reached Bai's study.

Ruoping knocked on the door.

'Come in.'

Ruoping and Chengyan stepped inside. It was an old-fashioned study. The window opposite the door was closed but its yellow curtains were open; in front of the window was a desk, on which lay a

41

laptop, documents and books, all bathed in the yellow light from a desk lamp. Beside the desk was a small round table, on which sat a coffee machine.

Two movable bookshelves full of Chinese and English books occupied the east and west walls up to the ceiling. Apparently the bookshelves were running out of space, for more books were stacked in the corners of the study.

Ruoping surveyed the bookshelves, looking for familiar names and titles. The professor, standing beside the coffee machine, gave Ruoping a welcoming smile before he noticed Chengyan.

'Ah, wait a second.' Bai walked back to the desk, sat on the office chair, and opened the drawer.

'I thought you put all DVDs in the movie room,' said Ruoping.

'I put the one he wanted right here in case I forgot. One forgets things easily at my age. For example, I left my car key on the work table in the garage this morning and it's still there…here it is!' Bai took out a DVD from the drawer and handed it to Chengyan, who thanked him with a slight nod and left.

Bai leant back in the chair with his hands clasped behind his neck. 'Now let's get down to business.'

Ruoping nodded and sat down on the sofa opposite the desk.

Bai began: 'What we're going to discuss is the tragedy last year. Maybe you've done some research… ah, help yourself to the coffee. It's fresh.'

'Thanks…I have done some research, but it'd be good if you could help me with the details.'

'Perfect. Then let's start from the very beginning. As you know, my older brother Jingfu Bai once owned one of the most famous motor companies in Taiwan. He commissioned a renowned architect to build the House of Rain after making his fortune, intending to spend his retirement here. It was also intended as the place for Dad to enjoy his last days. Unfortunately, Mom died early and Dad became handicapped after a car accident and was confined to a wheelchair afterwards. Shortly after the family moved in, Dad passed away from stomach cancer. My brother always sighed over the unpredictability of life.'

'He set a great example of filial piety.'

Bai smiled bitterly. 'Which Dad never had enough time to enjoy.'

'I'm sorry to hear that,' said Ruoping. He continued after a short pause. 'Your brother had unique taste. I remember reading the news about the House of Rain. It's not easy to build a castle like this in the mountains. The architect must have faced considerable difficulties.' He poured himself a cup of coffee and took a sip.

'You're right. The architect was Shengfeng Shi, known for his unique artistic style. My brother had known him since university days. Shi majored in architecture, my brother in power engineering. They were not on close terms and would only meet at the annual alumni gathering. After Shi made his name, my brother always said that he would commission him one day.'

'Why did your brother choose the character *rain* for the design of this house?'

'Not many people know that he was not only an engineer but also a poet and essayist. After his wife and daughter went to bed he would often immerse himself in his writing.'

'He was also a man of letters.'

Bai seemed carried away by memories. 'He liked the imagery of rain, and thought it was great subject matter for writing poetry. The inspiration of this house came from the great poem "Rainy Night" by the ancient Chinese poet Shangyin Li. The idea is that, since the house is the materialization of rain, staying inside it means being bathed in the rain, which enables one to experience the rain itself more deeply. It might be too abstract to understand, but simply put, it's just a liking for rain. To improve the artistic conception of rain, dim lighting was installed throughout the house.'

To Ruoping, rain represented loneliness and sadness. Not many people liked rainy days except poets. The dim lights reflected the symbolic meaning of rain, epitomising the solitude in Jingfu Bai's heart.

'Poets are romantic souls. They fall in love easily.' Bai put his hands on the arms of the chair. 'I'm not saying that he did anything wrong, and it's not my intention to judge him. But the fact is that he fell in love with Shi's wife.'

'Interesting.'

'To be frank, his marriage was a tragedy. The couple had fights over almost everything. Jingfu eventually just stopped talking to his wife,' sighed the professor. 'His eloquence disappeared when the conversation shifted from business to marital relationships. What was worse, Yinghan, his wife, followed his example.'

So the successful entrepreneur had failed the test of marriage. Ruoping could see the sorrow in Bai's eyes.

'Once the construction of the House of Rain began, Jingfu drove there every now and then to inspect the progress. Shi would bring his wife Wenliu Pan to monitor the work. That was how my brother met her. At some point, he asked her out, and they started dating secretly. One month later, Yinghan learned about it and told Shi.'

'How did it all end?'

'Jingfu made a profound apology. Shi threatened to stop construction, but was persuaded to continue after getting handsome compensation. His wife never showed up on the project again. Yinghan never forgave my brother for the affair, but she didn't ask for a divorce because of their daughter and the huge fortune she continued to enjoy.

'After moving into the House of Rain, matters got worse. Jingfu was never home. He hung out with friends all the time. He lost confidence because he'd never experienced such a big frustration in his career. In her husband's absence, Yinghan found a new hobby—dating men online.'

Ruoping didn't comment, but waited for Bai to continue.

'I don't know what happened exactly. What I do know is that she invited men she met online to the House of Rain when my brother was away….

'That was how their lives were before they died. Everyone became more distant from each other in this huge house. The most miserable soul in this tragedy was my niece—Yuyun.' Bai sighed again. 'Home was not the best shelter for Yuyun. If she were still alive she would be twenty-four years old, two years older than Lingsha, with whom she got along pretty well, despite not seeing each other very often. That was because Yuyun needed a friend.

'Lingsha told me that her cousin didn't have a happy school life. She always looked miserable. Children from broken families are like that; they have twisted value systems and are disappointed with the world.'

'It's the children who are the victims.'

'Yuyun ran away from home after her father's affair. She took a train and came to our place without any luggage, crying…' Bai shook his head, poured himself a cup of coffee and gulped it down. 'Jingfu and Yinghan finally took her back. I was in no position to interfere so I just let her go.'

'A sensitive question: were you close to your brother?' asked Ruoping after a pause.

'We didn't see each other very often after senior high school. It was even more difficult for us to meet after we got married, because he lived in the north and I lived in the south.'

Ruoping nodded.

'Eventually the real tragedy occurred. It was on February the tenth last year. My wife and I had gone to Taitung that day. On our way back to Tainan, we dropped by the House of Rain because Lingsha had asked me to borrow some DVDs from Yuyun.

'It was already ten when we arrived here. My wife kept saying that I spoiled Lingsha because I could have dropped by some other time...' Bai's voice was full of sadness. 'I always ignored her advice. It's too late to regret it because she passed away last year.'

'I'm sorry.'

'Sorry for the digression.' The professor seemed to be on the brink of tears but quickly pulled himself together. 'As we arrived here we saw a man hurrying out of the house, his right hand swathed in bandages....'

With pain and grief Bai recounted how he found the bodies of the family members: Yuyun Bai, Jingfu Bai, and Yinghan Qiu. The whole family had been slaughtered.

'Before the police came, my wife and I stayed in the living room and kept an eye on the corridor in case anyone should try to escape from there. But we didn't see anyone. The image of the man with the bandage stayed in my mind....'

'You suspected he did it.'

'Yes. I reported him to the police. In fact I met him once at Yinghan's birthday party. He was her university classmate. The police finally located him. His name is Weiqun Yang. He worked in a private company and was Yinghan's ex-boyfriend. His alibi for February 10 was that he was at home. Since he lived alone, no one could confirm his story.'

'Are you sure he was the man you saw that night?'

'Quite sure. His right arm was bandaged because of a fight he'd been in a couple of days before the slaughter, so the police treated him as the main suspect.

'As for the forensic evidence, examination of my brother's fingernails and the wound on his wife's neck revealed that he'd strangled her to death and had been killed in turn with the hatchet which had been dropped on the floor. He'd received at least seven blows, several of which were inflicted after he was dead.'

'Blows after death?'

'Exactly. The motive was officially unknown, but it was undoubtedly extreme hatred. Another thing to note is that the three died within half an hour of each other: my brother killed his wife, before being killed by a third person, who killed Yuyun afterwards.'

'Yuyun....'

Bai's face was shadowed with grief. 'She was raped after she died.'

'Poor girl.'

'The DNA tests showed that the seminal fluid in Yuyun's body had come from Yang. Also, his fingerprints were on the hatchet. He'd claimed innocence until the police found a pendant at his place that contained a photo of Yuyun and Lingsha. The Philippine maidservant working in the House of Rain testified that Yuyun always wore that pendant, which was missing from the crime scene. By the way, the maidservants had had the day off and were not in the house that night.'

'What did Yang say in the face of the evidence against him?'

'He finally admitted that he'd met Yinghan that night. They knew my brother would be away.'

'Sorry for interrupting. When did the two resume the relationship?'

'According to Yuyun's diary, the two had come into contact again after Yinghan had begun dating men online. Yang would come to the House of Rain when Jingfu wasn't home. The affair had lasted for at least a year.'

'That was not good for Yuyun.'

'Of course not: I'd been worried about her at the time. Yuyun and Lingsha had kept in contact online. Yuyun would frequently complain about her mother.'

'I see. Please continue about what happened on the night of February tenth.'

'Where was I? Ah, Yang said that he'd arrived at the House of Rain at seven-fifty. He'd opened the front door with a duplicate key, and gone upstairs to meet Yinghan. They'd had fun, and then Yang, fumbling for his new cell phone because he wanted to take a photo of Yinghan, had realised he'd left it in the car.

'He'd gone back to the car right away, but it had taken him a while to find the cell phone under the driver's seat. It was already nine by the time he'd got back to the house. He'd gone upstairs using the south staircase and noticed that there were footprints all the way up. As soon as he'd reached the first floor he'd seen Yuyun's body. He'd recognized Yuyun's face because he'd seen her frequently when he visited Yinghan. Seeing light coming out of my brother's room, he'd braced himself before entering the room, only to find Yinghan lying naked and dead on the bed, and a man lying on the floor, his head crushed…the scene was almost the same as when I'd found it.'

'The only difference was….'

'The only difference was that Yang had picked up the hatchet on the floor, inflicted several blows to my brother's head, left the room, and done to Yuyun's body what only a beast would have done. He'd taken Yuyun's pendant as a souvenir. He was inhuman!'

The professor suppressed his rising fury with difficulty. 'Yang said he'd been wanting to beat my brother since Jingfu took Yinghan from him; and he'd felt strong lust for Yuyun from the moment he'd first seen her.'

'The police didn't believe him.'

'No.' Bai gave a feeble smile. 'All the evidence was against him. What's more, all the blows at Jingfu's head had not been inflicted with typical male force. This accorded with the fact that Yang wouldn't have been able to use his full strength with that wounded arm.

'The prosecutor's reconstruction of the case was as follows. My brother had suspected Yinghan of adultery, so he'd decided to catch her in the act. He'd pretended to leave the house but had gone back without anyone noticing. He hadn't bothered to dry his shoes but had gone straight upstairs. He'd waited until Yang had left to get his cell phone, then entered the room and strangled Yinghan. While he was outside, Yang had noticed my brother's car in the woods and realised things had gone wrong. He'd taken the hatchet and the fishing line from the stockroom, gone back to the room and killed my brother. Yuyun had heard them fighting and come out to see what was happening. Yang had strangled her with the fishing line on the staircase.'

'Interesting. I have two questions. First, how did Yang know that the hatchet and the fishing line were in the stockroom? Second, why did he pick two murder weapons instead of one?'

'Good questions. The answer to the first might be that he hadn't had any particular weapon in mind and just stumbled over those two. As for the second question, it might be that he'd already decided to hush Yuyun but had somehow chosen a different weapon.'

47

'It's hard to believe he could just have stumbled over two deadly weapons in such a big house.'

'According to the Philippine maidservant, it wasn't really all that easy to locate the hatchet and the fishing line in the stockroom, because they had both been carefully put away. Those who believed Yang claimed that the real murderer had prepared the weapons beforehand. However, not many people believed that theory.'

'Did Yang leave any footprints in the house?'

'No. He'd worn indoor slippers in the house. The only footprints found were my brother's.'

'How about outside? No footprints either?'

'If there were any they would have been wiped out by the rain.'

'Any trace of break-in?'

'No. And there weren't even any suspicious fingerprints on the crime scene. All this made Yang even more suspect. People believed he'd lied to the police. He'd been frank about what he'd done to the bodies, probably because he couldn't challenge the strong evidence against him. If Yang was not the murderer, then it must have been....'

'Shengfeng Shi, the architect.'

Shi would be a good candidate, thought Ruoping, for his wife had had an affair with Jingfu Bai. Shi could have sneaked into the House of Rain on purpose to murder the unfortunate entrepreneur and accidentally witnessed him killing his unfaithful wife. How ironic...but was it Shi?

'Shi had an unbreakable alibi.' The professor's words interrupted Ruoping's thoughts. 'He was with his wife at a birthday party in Taipei from eight to eleven that night, so the police struck him off the list of suspects.'

'Who else had a motive?'

'My brother had a couple of business competitors but none of them could've committed the crime. Yang was still the major suspect. He lost his mind and hanged himself with his bedcover in the detention centre. Case closed.'

Bai took a gulp of coffee. It was ten-fifteen according to the clock on the wall.

'After that,' the professor continued, 'the House of Rain remained unoccupied until this winter. I hired new maidservants to clean the house—of course not the whole house but only the space we would use, as we only intended to use the house for vacation purposes.

'Shi contacted me after he heard that I was planning to re-open the house. He said he could do some maintenance for me. He was sorry for what had happened and would be happy to do something. I agreed. We moved in last week. This house was partly the brainchild of my brother, so I'm not going to sell it until I find someone who will appreciate it and take care of it.'

'Let's come straight to the point. You don't think Yang was the murderer, do you?'

'I never said that. The police could well be right. Anyway, the reason I asked you over is that I received a strange email two weeks ago.'

'Email?'

'Have a look for yourself.' Bai waved Ruoping to the laptop.

The screen showed an email sent on January twenty-seventh, headed *The Identity of the Real Murderer.* There was only one line in the email:

Sent from: (5,3)(8,3)(6,1)(5,2)(1,1)(6,2) (8,3)/ (6,3)(1,2)(6,1).

'Looks like a code,' said Ruoping. 'It could be the name of the sender.'

'Actually I want you to see the attachments.'

Bai clicked open the first attachment.

It was a photograph. A man in a black coat lay on the floor with his limbs spread out. His face had been beaten beyond recognition, and was covered with blood, hair and body tissue.

It was the body of Jingfu Bai.

8 *(February 10, 9.10 p.m.)*

Xiangya Yue's room was on the west side of the second floor, the second from the end of the corridor; the third room was occupied by Tingzhi Yan. There was no light coming from under Tingzhi's door. She was probably out.

Empty corridor, dim light.

Not only was Yunxin Liu insane, but so was she.

Xiangya took her clothes and toiletries from her suitcase and went to the bathroom. She was worn out.

After putting her stuff on the rack, she stepped into the bathtub, drew the curtain, and opened the shower nozzle.

The temperature of the water gradually rose. She felt relaxed.

After washing her hair, she soaped herself all over, which gave her the chance to study her body.

She was short but full-breasted. She was already accustomed to men's ogling looks.

There were several burns around her left nipple, which reminded her of Yunxin and the fiery encounter in her bedroom three months ago.

'You think you're beautiful, don't you?' Yunxin had asked her.

The arrogant face, the cold smile, and the hand holding a cigarette...all attributes of the queen.

Xiangya had lowered her head.

'Everyone says you're like a doll in a showcase. Everyone likes you. You have a lot of friends and you're a good pianist. You're beautiful and talented!'

Xiangya had been wary of the words and had stiffened.

'God is unfair. You're lucky because he gave you everything.'

She'd fought back the urge to reply. She knew many people were jealous of her. But their eyes only saw the surface and were blind to her defects.

'I can't deny you're adorable. But that very fact upsets me,' the other woman had continued coldly, as she sat in the chair opposite with her legs crossed, staring at her.

Xiangya had continued to stare down at the floor.

'Why does everyone make friends with you but not with me? Why does everyone think highly of you but not of me?'

Did everyone do that? Even if they did, that had nothing to do with her.

'You don't know my pain because you're a princess.'

'What do you want?' She'd had to use her full strength to force the words out.

'What do I want?' Yunxin had replied, with a chilling smile. 'I want you to be my friend and share everything with me.'

'What do you mean?'

'Be my slave.'

'No way!'

She had shouted without thinking. It had been a mistake.

Yunxin's smile had vanished. 'I'll let everyone know your secret if you disobey—what you did with *him*. Think about the consequences.'

Xiangya had looked up. If she could have stood back at that moment and looked at herself, what would she have seen? An angry doll? She had clenched her fists....

'Angry, huh? That won't help. *He* doesn't care if the whole world knows it. But you care, because you're a celebrity....'

Tears had welled up in Xiangya's eyes and everything had become blurred. She'd suddenly realised the whole thing had been a trap set by Yunxin.

'Take off your clothes.'

'...'

'I won't say it again.'

Hesitantly, she'd begun unbuckling her dress, hands trembling.

The other woman's smile had grown even colder.

Tears, so hot....

'What are you waiting for? Take them off.'

After she'd finished, the ice queen had held the cigarette up in her hand again.

'Good. Next, the mark of friendship....'

The fiery eyes had drawn closer.

The hot water from the shower nozzle scalded her skin, which reminded her that she was taking a shower in the House of Rain.

She sighed, turning the tap to adjust the temperature.

Why had she allowed herself to suffer?

Good question. Was it because she feared the consequences, or because she was a coward—too cowardly to make a choice?

There was a storm outside, and also one raging inside her.

A moment later she was sitting on the edge of the bed, done with skincare.

As she was about to sort out her luggage, there was a knock on the door.

'Who is it?'

No response.

She remained seated, gazing at the doorknob.

Dead silence for thirty seconds.

She rose, went to the door, and looked through the peephole.

There was no one there.

She unbolted the door and opened it.

There was a white piece of paper lying folded on the floor.

She picked it up and looked around. There was still no one there and all the doors on the corridor were closed.

Her heart beat faster. She closed the door, leant back against it, took a deep breath and unfolded the note.

It was the kind of notepaper that was in every guest room. The handwriting was scratchy.

See you in the library at ten. Please come, for my sake.
Chengyan

She folded the note and looked at her watch. Fifteen minutes to go.

Why had he asked her to meet? Should she go?

His face came to her: handsome but melancholy, sombre as a statue when he was silent, but brightening when a subject interested him.

She didn't know much about him. Come to think of it, she didn't know much about anyone, even her family. But she did have a good impression of him....

And Chengyan liked her. She knew that much. He'd asked her out several times but she hadn't accepted, because she'd been tied up with Yunxin's poodle.

God was fair. She was good-looking but she was miserable.

Perhaps Chengyan could save her.

But first the evidence in Yunxin's hands had to be destroyed. Even that might not be enough. Both Yunxin and her poodle may have to be destroyed as well.

52

She put on a white cotton dress and left the room.

All the curtains along the corridor were drawn. The howling storm outside contrasted starkly with the dead silence inside.

She passed Tingzhi's room, the west staircase, two empty rooms and the public shower room and turned right onto the corridor leading to the library.

In the middle of the corridor was another one to the left, leading to more guest rooms and the north staircase; to the right was a set of double-doors, behind which was the corridor leading to the Bais' rooms.

She kept walking straight ahead until she reached the heavy double-doors of the library. She pushed them open and went in.

There was a scholarly atmosphere inside, as if the books were alive and met there for conferences.

Apart from the shelves crammed full of books, there were a few round tables and study desks with lamps.

Only one of the lamps was on. The light came from a study desk on the right near the only window on the west wall.

A figure rose against the light, giving Xiangya a start.

'Thanks for coming,' said a calm, familiar voice.

'Why did you want to see me?' She looked around uneasily.

Chengyan pointed to a chair beside one of the round tables, on which were a dark bottle and two wine glasses. 'Have a seat.'

Xiangya hesitated, then sat down. Chengyan sat down opposite her. 'I just want to talk to you,' he said.

'Talk? Why now and why here?'

'No one will disturb us here. This is a quiet place.'

He poured some wine into the glasses.

'Red wine. Your favourite.'

Studying the wine in the glass, she started to relax. Chengyan's expression triggered something in her heart.

'Did you buy this?' she asked softly.

'It's from the kitchen. Lingsha told us to help ourselves to any of the food and drink. Try it.' He took a sip.

Xiangya followed suit. The wine had a mellow taste.

Chengyan put down the glass and looked at her thoughtfully. 'How did things go today?' His eyes were like diamonds in the half-light.

'Not so badly.' She met his gaze but then turned away.

He sighed, placing his right hand on the table, and began to make lengthy and impassioned comments about the huge house and the weather. Xiangya listened quietly as she sipped her wine; somehow she was enjoying the moment—the talk, the man, the atmosphere.

After a while he stopped and studied her intently.

'In fact, I want to ask you something about Yunxin Liu.'

Just as she'd expected. The sense of unease returned.

'What about her?'

She clenched her fists on her thighs.

'I want to know more about what happened between the two of you.'

'I don't feel like talking about it.'

Silence.

Chengyan sighed again and frowned.

'Do you know something? You've changed a lot.' He raised his voice and appeared somewhat agitated. 'You used to be sunny, but now you are gloomy. You're Yunxin's slave.'

Without warning she felt giddy and her head felt heavy....

'I just want to help.'

As if in a trance, she saw him stand up and tower over her like a dark shadow.

Xiangya lifted herself up using the edge of the table.

'Sit down, Ya. Sit down.'

His tone changed completely when he addressed her by her nickname. It was tender, soft, and...dangerous.

He stepped forward, holding out both hands.

Xiangya felt weak, as if all of her strength had been stolen. The wine she had drunk....

There was no time to think. She turned and ran through the open library doors.

Out in the corridor, she stumbled along with all her remaining strength. Desperately, she reached the double-doors leading south to the family's private quarters.

Pushing them open, she continued her escape. There were rooms on both sides of the corridor. At the end she turned right without thinking too much, only to find yet another set of double-doors in front of her....

Chengyan was right behind her and her limbs were getting feebler.

Pushing open this latest set of doors, she saw a staircase in front of her, leading downstairs. There was a small room next to it.

The door of the room was closed, but she lunged for it and groped for the knob.

It opened easily and Xiangya stepped inside. The light was on. There were things scattered around on the floor, but she was too weak to pay attention.

She closed the door, locked it quickly and looked around for the light switch. Chengyan would be able to find her by the light coming from under the door, so she had to turn it off.

No sooner had she pressed one of the two buttons on the wall than she heard Chengyan's voice just outside the room.

'I saw you go in. Come out, Ya.'

Everything she saw became blurred. She felt dizzier than ever.

Suddenly terror took hold of her, not because she couldn't escape from the man outside, but because she had just caught a glimpse of something on the floor.

A saw....

9 *(February 10, 10.25 p.m.)*

Ruoping averted his eyes from the photo.

'The other was the photo of Yinghan's body,' said Bai gloomily. It must have been very difficult for him to see the bodies again.

The professor clicked open the second photo and closed it after Ruoping had taken a quick look.

'Any idea who sent this?'

'You wouldn't be here if I knew that.'

It seemed that the professor didn't smoke; otherwise a cigarette might have helped. He gulped down his cup of coffee.

'What do you think about this email, professor?'

'This is just my guess…judging from the title, someone doesn't think that Yang was responsible for the murder. This person was probably close to Yang. The purpose of sending me the photos was to urge me to find the truth.'

'I wonder if the sender has evidence that can prove Yang's innocence.'

'I don't think so; otherwise he or she would have given it to the police.'

'That makes sense. But why you?'

Bai's face turned grim. 'Maybe the sender thinks Yang died partly because of my testimony. Moreover, I have to admit that I did publicly denounce him as a brutal killer, because at that time I really thought he'd done it…come to think of it, the sender might be giving me a chance to make amends for what I did.'

'Well, Yang could still very well be the murderer.'

'I know. But now I see a need to reinvestigate.'

'But I don't see there's much chance. The key clues—if there were any—have probably all gone.'

'You're using the subjunctive mood. That's the point.'

'Whatever.'

'The other thing is, I hope you can also find out who sent the email.'

'I believe the police will be able to work that out very quickly. They have the technology.'

'I don't want to expose this person through the police because I believe he or she is close to Yang, for whose death I feel partly responsible. As I said, if the sender really held any key evidence, he or she would already have offered it to the police. So even if the police did unmask this person, it wouldn't help with the case.'

'I see,' said Ruoping. Then, after a long pause, 'I'll do my best.'

'You'll get paid regardless of the result.'

'Money doesn't really matter. I just want you to know that I can't guarantee what will transpire.'

'I understand. But I'm counting on you.'

'All right. Let's start by working out who the sender is. If we can find out where it was sent—.'

Suddenly they heard someone knocking rapidly on a door somewhere, mixed with the sounds of shouting.

The two listened attentively.

'It's not this door. I think it's the one outside.' The professor eyed Ruoping, who nodded.

The shouts started again more loudly, and this time they could make out the words.

'Open the door, Ya!'

'Isn't that Chengyan's voice?' said Ruoping.

'Sounds like him. Why is he knocking?'

'I'll check.' Ruoping stood up.

'I'm going with you.'

Ruoping opened the door of the study and found a thin figure standing beside the set of double-doors on the left. The right door of the two was open inwards.

It was Lingsha. She was in white trousers and a blue coat, her long hair tied back in a bow.

'What's going on, Lingsha?' Bai frowned. 'Why are you standing there? Who's knocking?'

'I left my room to see what happened. It's Chengyan.'

Lingsha stepped aside to let Ruoping and her father pass through the open door.

A tall, thin figure stood before the closed door of the room next to the stairway. He kept hitting the door with his fists.

'What are you doing?'

Chengyan turned towards Ruoping, his eyes mixed with frenzy and anguish.

'Xiangya locked herself in.'

'Why is she in there?' asked Bai.

'She ran inside and locked the door, and now refuses to come out.'

'I can see that. But my question was why did she go in there in the first place?'

'Well...' Chengyan scowled. 'I'll tell you later. Now let's get her out! I'm worried about her!'

Before anyone could respond, he snarled and kicked the door. Bai sprang at him and took his arms; Ruoping dashed forward and gave the professor a hand.

'What are you doing?' Bai gasped.

'Sorry.' Chengyan jerked himself free, turning to face the window on the south wall. 'I am just...too worried about her. Can't someone get the key and unlock it?'

'I don't see any keyhole,' said Ruoping to Bai. 'What's wrong with this door?'

'Don't ask me. That's the design. Quite a few doors in this house are like that. You can't expect everything to make sense with all this *avant-garde* architecture.'

'Looks as though the only way to get in is to break it down!' All of a sudden, Chengyan threw himself fiercely at the door again, almost hitting the professor.

The crazed man began beating and kicking at the door, apparently out of his mind, because some of his kicks landed on the button and the doorframe. The professor and Ruoping dragged him back again.

'Calm down! Let's use a tool to break in,' shouted Bai. 'Give me a second. I'll go and find something!'

So saying, the professor left and Ruoping tried the door again. It was definitely locked.

It would normally have been a good opportunity to ask Chengyan about what exactly had happened before they arrived, but Ruoping remained silent because he knew the man wouldn't speak until they'd got Xiangya Yue out.

Lingsha had been standing by the double-doors, watching them. Though she remained outwardly composed, there was uneasiness in her eyes.

After a few minutes Bai returned with a hatchet, which he handed to Chengyan.

A hole soon appeared in the middle of the thin door and, after a dozen more critical blows, Chengyan was able to put his hand through and open it.

What happened next was totally unexpected. Chengyan jerked backwards and fell to the floor as if knocked down by an invisible fist. The hatchet fell from his grasp.

He seemed to have been shocked by something in the room.

Ruoping and Bai both reached the door at the same time.

The light inside was on.

'Good grief,' exclaimed Bai, his face turning deathly pale. 'Don't look, Lingsha. Stay away.'

Though the light inside was dim, Ruoping could see that there were no windows in the room. Several objects lying on the floor emphasized the bareness of the room: an empty clothes stand with a round base circled by a fishing line; a saw with red stains lying beside the door; and a body lying prone in a pool of blood... presumably female, to judge by the dress.

The blood came from a wide gap in the neck where the head should have been. The cross-section was uneven and tainted with crimson. The head was not in the room.

Ruoping turned desperately to Chengyan and asked: 'Are you sure Xiangya Yue entered this room?'

'Absolutely,' replied the other, staring in disbelief at the floor. 'That's her dress.'

'You heard her locking the door, and you waited outside.'

'Yes.'

'No one came in or out of the room?'

'What's the point of these stupid questions? I'm the only one here!' The young man sat down on the floor, buried his face in his hands and began wailing.

'Impossible,' said Bai in a trembling voice. 'This is *impossible!*'

Ruoping bit his lip and gazed at the bloody scene.

The rain outside continued to pour relentlessly down.

Chapter 2
Night of Beheading

10 *(February 10, 10.50 p.m.)*

Lingsha took a deep breath and tried to pull herself together.

The door of death was closed. Ruoping stood by the door, a handkerchief in his right hand. At first she thought he needed the handkerchief to wipe away his perspiration, but soon realised she was wrong when Ruoping said, 'Let's get out of here. We'd better not touch anything on the crime scene.'

'We should call the police,' said Bai, his pale complexion flecked with blood.

'We should, but I doubt they can make it here. Anyway, after you call the police, could you ask everyone to assemble in the living room?'

'Assemble everyone...? Yes, of course.'

'Another thing, is there a key to that set of double-doors behind you? I want to lock it to prevent anyone from getting in and out via the staircase.'

'There is a key. I'll get it.'

'Wait a minute,' said Lingsha. 'Let's do things separately. You call the police and I'll get everyone to assemble in the living room.'

'Come to think of it,' said Bai, 'I should do that because the murderer might still be around. You go to my study, call the police and get the key for Ruoping.'

'But....'

'Just do it. Don't waste time.'

'Your father is right. Just do it,' said the young scholar.

'If you say so.'

Lingsha went back to her father's study.

She still couldn't accept the brutal fact that her friend was already dead. She was too shocked to cry, and there was no time for her to grieve.

After entering the study she picked up the phone by the desk and made a call.

The next ten minutes were among the most frustrating moments in her life. The policeman who answered the phone had never heard of the House of Rain and didn't know where it was. She gave him the address and waited for him to make a couple of calls. Then he told her that the police wouldn't be able to get there until the landslide had been cleared. The rainstorm had been causing havoc in many of the mountain villages and a lot of people had been killed.

Under the circumstances, the police could only give her some instructions about safety and how to preserve the crime scene, including the suggestion of taking photos of the body. As she put down the phone, Ruoping appeared in the doorway.

'I asked Bingyu Xu to help Chengyan to walk downstairs because he could barely walk...what did the police say?'

She briefed him on what had happened.

'As I expected. Now please get me the key and the camera. I'll take photos.'

Lingsha opened one of the desk drawers and took out a camera; she opened another and produced a bunch of keys with identifying stickers and handed keys and camera to the young academic.

'Thanks. Now go and wait in the living room. I'll be there soon.'

So saying, Ruoping left the study.

Lingsha was alone now and was suddenly seized by sadness. She spent a moment getting a grip of herself and wiping away some late tears. Ten minutes later she walked out of the study.

As she passed the half-closed double-doors, she saw Ruoping in the room, squatting down, checking the body.

The bloody scene came to mind again. She suppressed the thought and went downstairs using the north staircase.

A few moments later she was in the living room. Her appearance caused a small commotion. Her father showed relief on seeing her and waved her to sit down. She took a seat next to Tingzhi and briefly surveyed the small crowd.

Everyone was here except Ruoping.

'We'll wait here until Ruoping arrives,' announced the professor. 'Please don't leave the room.'

'What happened exactly?' shouted Bingyu angrily. 'It's very late. And what's wrong with Chengyan? Why does he look so pale? He's keeping his mouth shut like a clam!'

'I'm really sorry. Something serious has happened. I'll explain later.'

Bingyu looked around, paying no attention. 'Where is Xiangya?'

Lingsha saw her father approaching her. He whispered: 'What did the police say?'

'They can't make it at the moment.'

'No surprise.'

Bingyu suddenly lunged at Chengyan, grasped his shoulders and shook him.

'You must know something! Is Xiangya all right?'

'Leave him alone! Stop behaving like a child!' Lingsha raised her voice.

He released his hands and turned towards her. Their eyes met. After a moment Bingyu looked away, cursed and returned to his seat.

Lingsha saw her father giving her an approving nod.

It seemed a long wait. But maybe she had lost her sense of time and it was shorter than she thought. She wondered why her father had counted so much on Ruoping. He was just a philosophy professor, after all....

Just as her thoughts were starting to wander, the young man appeared.

'Sorry for keeping you waiting.' Ruoping walked to the centre of the living room, tipping the silver-framed glasses resting on his nose, his manner refined, elegant, and gentle. 'I have bad news for you.'

Tingzhi asked in a calm voice: 'We are all at a loss. Please tell us what's going on.'

'I will. But be prepared for the worst.' His eyes sought everyone in the room. 'Xiangya Yue is dead.'

The atmosphere in the living room changed, as if there were also a storm inside.

'Xiangya is dead?' Bingyu stared in disbelief.

'Strictly speaking, I can't be sure yet that the body we found is hers, although the dress certainly is.'

'What? What do you mean?'

'The body's head is missing.'

There was consternation in the room. Yunxin turned as pale as a dead fish; Bingyu's mouth was hanging open.

'We need to confirm the victim's identity,' said Ruoping. 'Can anyone help us?'

There was a long silence before someone finally spoke.

'There's a scar on the back of her left hand,' said Chengyan in a flat voice.

63

'A knife wound?'

Chengyan nodded slightly.

'I noticed that scar when examining the body. Do you know how she got the wound?'

Someone gasped, but Lingsha couldn't tell who; at the same time Chengyan said: 'She got that wound not long ago when cutting vegetables.'

'Is that what she told you?'

'Yes.'

'All right. I think we can all agree on the victim's identity. Now I'll explain what happened.'

Ruoping briefly recounted how they found the body.

'I don't get it,' said Bingyu, holding an unlit cigarette. 'Why did Xiangya enter that room? Why was Chengyan there? You didn't explain anything!'

'Chengyan can tell you, but I don't think he's in the mood to talk about it for now. I have something else to announce.'

Lingsha knew what it was, and knew it would cause a big commotion.

'The police said that they can't make it here until the landslide has been cleared up.'

'What?' exclaimed Bingyu.

His exclamation triggered the expected commotion.

'All this is unexpected,' said Lingsha's father. 'Before the police arrive, please cooperate and follow Ruoping's instructions....'

'Bullshit!' shouted the playboy.

As Lingsha was about to defend her father, she realized Bingyu's target was Ruoping.

'Who the hell is this guy?' he said disdainfully. 'Why should we listen to him? He is a scholar, not a detective!'

'He is a detective,' said Bai.

Detective! Lingsha herself was surprised. Come to think of it, the way he examined the body was indeed like a detective.

'Although he's an amateur, Ruoping has helped the police solve several major cases. I asked him over to reinvestigate my brother's case. But since we are all now involved in this new murder, shall we just entrust this case to him?'

'Ridiculous!' Bingyu jumped up from his chair and thundered:

'He's neither a policeman nor a certified private detective! I'd rather risk my life leaving here than entrust the case to this amateur!'

'Please believe me, I have complete confidence in him,' said Lingsha's father, with authority.

'I'll speak for myself.'

Ruoping walked slowly towards Bingyu. He remained composed and calm, while the other's eyes remained hostile.

'You can leave if you want. But no one will lend you their car. And, you'll become the main suspect if you are so desperate to leave.'

'I didn't kill anyone.'

'You'll need to prove your innocence. Let's investigate and see whether we can solve the case before the police arrive.'

'Why should I listen to you?'

'Then feel free to leave.' The detective turned and walked back to where he'd been standing.

All eyes were on Bingyu. Under everyone's gaze, he struggled to say something but failed and withdrew into sullen silence.

After a moment of silence, the owner of the house asked: 'What do we do now, Ruoping?'

'I want to start by checking everyone's alibi.'

11 *(February 10, 11.40 p.m.)*

The word "alibi" hung like a cloud over the room.

Ruoping surveyed everyone. Some avoided his eyes; some met his gaze, one of whom was Tingzhi Yan.

'We need to know the time of death first,' she said.

'That's right. Chengyan might know the answer because he was the last one who saw Xiangya Yue alive.'

All eyes turned to the downcast young man, who looked up defiantly. Ruoping had assumed his eyes would be red from grief, but they weren't.

'Can you answer my questions?'

Chengyan nodded slowly and disconsolately.

'Fine. So the first question is: why was Xiangya in that room?'

'I don't know.'

'Did you ask her to meet you?'

There was a pause before the answer came. 'Yes, but not there.'

'Where did you meet?'

'In the library.'

Ruoping nodded. He took out a small notepad and a pen from the pocket of his black trousers and recorded what Chengyan had just said.

'When did you meet?' he continued.

'At ten o'clock.'

'What happened then?'

'We had a drink and a chat.'

'What kind of drink?'

'Red wine.' Chengyan appeared alert when responding.

'Where did you get the wine?'

'I asked her and she got the bottle ready for me.' He nodded at Cindy, who was sitting in the corner with Ru.

Ruoping turned towards the nervous maidservant and asked softly: 'Cindy, is what this gentleman just said correct?'

Cindy looked quickly from Ruoping to Chengyan. 'Yes,' she said in a timid voice.

'Did you bring it to the library?'

'No. Mr. Fang said he'd do it himself.'

66

Ruoping nodded and turned to Chengyan again. 'Why didn't you let Cindy do it?'

'Why should I?' The other raised his voice.

'When was the wine ready?'

The young man paused before answering. 'A couple of minutes before ten.'

'Is that right, Cindy?'

'Yes.'

Ruoping turned to Chengyan. 'Why did Xiangya leave the library?'

'She ran out suddenly.'

'Suddenly? Why?'

'I've no idea.' His face twitched slightly.

'And you went after her.'

'Yes.'

'Did you follow her all the way to the staircase?'

'Yes.'

'Did you see her enter the small room next to the stairs?'

He nodded.

'Are you certain that the person entering the room was Xiangya Yue? Did you see her face at that very moment?'

Chengyan appeared confused about Ruoping's question. 'What are you talking about? I'd been following her!'

'I just wanted to make sure.' Ruoping took notes and continued: 'Then you waited there until the professor and I arrived?'

'You know the answer, don't you?'

'Thank you for your cooperation. That's all for now.' Ruoping turned to Bai. 'Professor, do you know what the room where we found Xiangya is used for? It's windowless.'

'I suppose it's a stockroom but I'm not sure.' Bai frowned. 'There are so many rooms in this house and many of them are empty. We just moved in and haven't had time to clean all the rooms. As I said, this is a strange house and some designs just don't make sense. I'd say it's the designer's aesthetics.'

'I see. Now I have some questions for Lingsha.'

The girl raised her head in mild surprise.

'Yes?'

'Earlier you mentioned that you'd left your room to check what was happening, because you'd heard strange sounds?'

'As I was about to turn in at ten twenty-five I heard footsteps. I opened the door and saw two figures passing by one after another. I put on my coat and went over to the double-doors opposite my father's room. Then you arrived.'

'What did you see before we arrived?'

'Chengyan was knocking on the door of the small room, as you know.'

'Did you see anyone leaving the room Xiangya had gone into before we arrived?'

'No.'

'Did Chengyan do anything except knock?'

'No.'

'Are you sure that they both went through the double-doors?'

'Yes.'

'I don't understand,' Chengyan cut in impatiently. 'What's the point of all these trivial questions? It just seems a waste of time.'

'No. These questions are all very important,' said Tingzhi calmly. 'The implication of these questions is surprising.'

'That is the crux of this murder,' said Ruoping. 'As some of you might have noticed... the only entrance to the crime scene was locked from the inside and watched from the outside. Yet, miraculously, the killer, along with the head of the victim, disappeared from the sealed space.'

12 *(February 10, 11.50 p.m.)*

Renze Bai tried to suppress the spreading feeling of unease.

He'd been suffering from headaches since his brother's death, and it had worsened after his wife had passed away. The doctor had said it was all psychological.

His head was buzzing like a malfunctioning machine. The image of the headless body was stuck in his mind, more shocking even than the three bodies he'd seen last year....

'This is an impossible murder. I can't explain how the killer escaped from that room. It was locked from the inside,' said Ruoping.

There was a moment of silence in the living room.

'Are there any secret passages in the room?' asked Tingzhi. 'I wouldn't be surprised if there were, since this is such a strange house.'

The girl was brilliant, thought Bai. Tingzhi seemed to be the smartest among her daughter's classmates. He'd noticed she'd been observing everything very carefully. But he didn't understand why she was here. She didn't seem close to anyone. Had Lingsha invited her?

'I didn't find any secret doors in the room,' said Ruoping.

'My brother told me there were no secret passages in the house,' agreed Bai.

'Then how did the killer get out of the room?' asked Lingsha.

'We'll get to that later.' Ruoping referred to his notepad. 'Xiangya was found dead at ten-fifty, and she was last seen at roughly ten twenty-five. Though I'm no medical expert, I'm confident she died sometime between ten twenty-five and ten-thirty. Now I want to investigate everyone's alibi during that period of time.

'The professor and I were in the study at that time, and we were witnesses for each other. Lingsha testified that she saw Chengyan passing through the double-doors and a few seconds later she saw him standing in front of the room in question. Since he was only out of Lingsha's sight for a few seconds, he could well be innocent. As for Lingsha, no one can testify as to her whereabouts earlier, but she was with us from ten-thirty....'

'I think we need to look at the case from a different perspective,' said Tingzhi with a shrewd look in her eye. 'All the testimony says that nobody left the room after Xiangya went in. Doesn't that mean that no one was in the room when Xiangya was killed?'

'You mean—.'

'I mean either she committed suicide or there was a death trap inside the room. In the former case, alibis don't make any sense. In the latter case, the killer must have an alibi; otherwise there would be no point in setting the killing apparatus.'

Ruoping nodded. 'Good thinking. But then why did the killer go to all the trouble of making the whole thing look impossible? It's not necessary if all the killer wants is an alibi. Adding the element of impossibility only invites suspicion.'

'Perhaps the killer didn't anticipate that the room would be locked and watched.'

'I don't think your two hypotheses are convincing. If Xiangya committed suicide, how did she manage to behead herself? And without leaving the head in the room? If there were some kind of murderous trap, there should be some traces left on the scene, but I didn't find any.'

'There might be some traces, not that there should be,' smiled Tingzhi.

'We can't reach any conclusion unless there are more clues. We should continue investigating everyone's alibi,' smiled Ruoping in return.

There were no protests except for Bingyu's grumbling.

'Good,' said Ruoping. 'I hope everyone will agree that Professor Bai and I have a decent alibi. I'd say that Chengyan and Lingsha probably have, too. Now the next is…Miss Yan, could you tell us where you were at ten twenty-five?'

'I was here—in the living room,' said Tingzhi.

'Here? What were you doing?'

'I wanted to have a change of air, so I took a walk downstairs. The living room is a good place for meditation and that's why I was here.'

'Meditating on what?'

'That's my business.'

'Indeed. Did you notice anything unusual before everyone got here?'

'No.'

'Did you see anyone while you were in here?'

70

'No.'

'Thank you.' Ruoping turned to Bingyu. 'Now it's your turn.'

The playboy threw away the unlit cigarette and gave Ruoping a disdainful look. He claimed that he was eating in the dining room until everyone was called to the living room. Ru was his witness.

Ruoping nodded. 'So two more people are out.' He turned to Yunxin Liu. 'How about you?'

She bit her lip with a lingering fear in her eyes. 'I was in my room. That's all.'

'I see.'

Ruoping consulted his notes and asked. 'The only one left is Cindy. Cindy, where were you at ten twenty-five?'

'I...I am not sure of time.' The maidservant appeared uneasy.

'Then please tell me what you did after dinner.'

'I was...doing laundry.'

'Laundry?'

'Yes....'

'Where is the laundry?'

'In the back of the house, next to the north staircase.'

'Did you see anyone when you were there?'

She thought for a moment. 'No.'

'Are you sure?'

'Yes.' She turned her eyes away.

'That's all. Thank you.' Ruoping jotted down her words on his notepad.

'Have you reached any conclusion?' asked the professor.

The young man shook his head. 'Not yet. We need more clues.' He rose and began pacing up and down.

A thought suddenly occurred to Bai:

'By the way, the saw in that room... was that the murder weapon?'

'Good question.' Ruoping stopped. 'This is a very bizarre case. Aside from the locked-room situation, how the victim died also baffles me.'

'What do you mean?'

There was a heavy crash of thunder outside.

'Xiangya Yue's head was not sawn off. It was torn off.'

13 *(February 11, 12.30 a.m.)*

The house was now like an inescapable nightmare. Fear was everywhere, spreading in a hellish manner....

Ruoping could feel the malevolent air in the house. There seemed to be an invisible devil lurking in the place, mocking the rationality of which humans are so proud.

Something else had to be added to this hellish brew: the footsteps from the first floor he'd heard the night before.

He couldn't see enough light at this moment. Not enough.

Ruoping returned to the study with Bai after the meeting in the living room. Before dismissing everyone, he'd made an announcement: don't walk in the house alone, don't open your door to anyone who doesn't identify himself, and don't let anyone you don't know well enter your room....

A new day had just begun. Although he felt sleepy, Ruoping tried to focus his mind.

'What should we do now?' asked Bai. A new pot of coffee was placed before him. They definitely needed some strong coffee at this stage.

'I'm not sure. This case is highly unusual.'

'Do you think it's relevant to the one I asked you to investigate?'

'Possibly.'

'It's already past midnight, so it's already a new day...it occurred to me that yesterday was the tenth of February, the same date as the murders last year.'

Ruoping studied Bai closely before responding. 'I'm beginning to feel that the truth might go beyond any answer we can think of.'

'It could be just sheer coincidence. But if not, it would be hard to explain why Xiangya Yue would have anything to do with my brother's case.'

'We'll work that out later. For now, we have another task.' He took out his notepad and opened it to a specific page. 'Please take a look at this.'

After a brief look, Bai returned the notepad to Ruoping. 'I'm thinking that, but for Lingsha's testimony, Chengyan would've become the main suspect.'

Alibis
Time of death: Feb. 10: 10.25 to 10.30 p.m.

Name	Location	Witness
Ruoping Lin	In the study	Renze Bai
Renze Bai	As above	Ruoping Lin
Lingsha Bai	First in the room and then on the corridor	Ruoping Lin and Renze Bai (10.30)
Bingyu Xu	In the dining room	Ru
Chengyan Fang	On the corridor and then in the staircase	Lingsha Bai
Yunxin Liu	In her room	None
Tingzhi Yan	In the living room	None
Cindy	In the laundry	None
Ru	In the dining room	Bingyu Xu

Questions:
1. What's the motive? Does it have anything to do with Jingfu Bai's case? (Both happened on the tenth of February. Is that a coincidence?)
2. How did the killer get out of the locked room?
3. How and why did the killer take the body's head away?
4. How and why did the killer tear the victim's head off? (How much strength does one need to tear off a person's head?)
5. What's the reason for constructing a locked room? (Apparently not for framing anyone, or to create the false impression of suicide.)
6. Whodunit?

P.S. The body is in Xiangya Yue's dress and has a scar on its left hand. Chengyan testified that Xiangya bore such a scar.

'That's right. He would be the one who last saw the victim alive. I know what you mean. It could be that the killer intended to make Chengyan the scapegoat but failed, due to the unexpected involvement of Lingsha. But if that were the case, the murderer could have locked Chengyan in the room with Xiangya or made him find the body first.'

'Agreed.'

'It's a shame. I can't answer any of the questions I listed at this stage. What happened just doesn't make sense.'

Bai clasped his hands tightly until his knuckles turned white. 'If Chengyan didn't lie to us, the killer must have hidden in the room and somehow escaped without our notice after we broke in.'

'In that case the murderer must be a hollow man.'

'I admit it was a stupid suggestion.'

'Hard to say. Maybe there was some kind of trick.'

'So then, how did the murderer get out of the room?'

They looked at each other in silence.

'It's just occurred to me that there's one crucial point we haven't considered,' said Ruoping. 'And that's the possibility that the killer is someone from outside the house.'

'An intruder?'

'Exactly. So far there's no evidence for that, but we need to keep an eye out—.'

All of a sudden the door opened to reveal Lingsha standing there, panting, her cheeks turning pink.

'What's wrong?' asked Bai.

'Bingyu had decided to leave, using Chengyan's car, but the key's missing.'

14 *(Zhengyu Jiang's Soliloquy)*

The poor girl's head is still lying on the floor.

I didn't touch it. At first I'd thought about moving it into the room by the staircase instead of leaving the wretched thing just lying there. But then I changed my mind and just closed the door and left. I'd never seen a corpse in my life, and a chopped-off head was even more terrifying. The image of it kept intruding into my thoughts, making me shudder.

Xiangya seems to have been in great terror before she died. Her hair was spread over her face like the legs of a dying spider. It was a lonely head in a lonely space. So surreal.

I've been lying on the bed in my room, chewing over what Ruoping Lin just said in the living room. Not until then had I realised whose head it was. It wasn't easy to recognize that twisted face without any extra information.

I can't believe Xiangya is dead, decapitated.

Ruoping Lin said her head had been torn off, which chilled me to the bone. Three people had died last year in this same house, and now the curse of death has struck again. I feel terror-stricken on account of the bizarre murder, but I try to pull myself together.

I mustn't forget my purpose in coming here.

Nevertheless, I'm still troubled by the thought that there's a killer in the house. The killer could strike again, which would be a concern for me, for I won't be able to move around safely to carry out my plan.

What if I let others know I'd found Xiangya's head? Would that help with the case?

Not a good idea. That would hinder my plan. Yes, the plan. I have to stick to my plan even if there's been a murder here.

This is an adventure, a bold game. The way I play the game will be unique....

There's a sudden burst of sound. I sit up and listen.

15 *(February 11, 12.50 a.m.)*

On their way downstairs, Lingsha briefed Ruoping and her father on what had happened.

Following the meeting in the living room, she'd stayed behind to give the maidservants moral support, after which she'd left and gone upstairs via the north staircase. As she'd stepped out of the staircase on the second floor, she'd heard people arguing to her right, who turned out to be Bingyu and Chengyan.

'Someone's stolen it!' shouted Bingyu.

The angry young man walked straight past Lingsha without looking at her. He scurried into the corridor in front of the staircase and turned right before the double-doors.

'He wants to leave the house and asked for my car key,' said Chengyan miserably. 'But it's missing. He thinks someone has stolen it and has gone to sort things out.'

Lingsha hurried to the guest rooms on the west side with Chengyan and saw Bingyu shouting and knocking on everyone's door. Tingzhi and Yunxin both opened their doors, looking confused.

It turned out that no one knew where Chengyan's key was. Bingyu attempted to search their rooms but was rebuffed.

'The key could have been left in the living room,' scowled Bingyu. 'I'll go and find it!' He left abruptly.

'Let's check it out. I do wonder where it went,' said Tingzhi with interest. She followed Bingyu out.

Chengyan hesitated, but soon moved in the same direction.

After the three had gone downstairs, Lingsha went to her father's study to report what had happened. Ruoping and Bai decided to follow Bingyu and the others to make sure things didn't go wrong. Lingsha went with them.

As they reached the ground floor by the north staircase, they saw Ru standing anxiously beside the stairs.

'They've checked the living room, dining room and recreation room. Now they're in the garage.'

'Thank you,' said Bai. 'We'll handle this. Go back to your room and have a good sleep.'

The three moved to the west side of the house.

They passed the movie room, the table tennis room, and the west staircase. The door at the end of the west corridor led to the garage. Ruoping pushed it open.

The light in the garage was on. Bingyu was standing beside Chengyan's car; the latter was sitting on the floor with his arms around his knees; Tingzhi, in a T-shirt and jeans, crossing her arms across her chest, looked at them coolly.

'Finally you're all here,' she said.

'Have you found the key?' asked Ruoping.

'No.'

'Why are you here with them?'

'I'm just curious.'

Ruoping said to Bingyu: 'How were you planning to leave after you find the key? There's a landslide.'

'Better than staying here!' the other barked in reply, his messy blonde hair covering his brow. 'Three people died last year, and now someone's head was torn off. Anyone with a grain of common sense would get out of this crazy place!'

'We don't know whether the killer will strike again or not. I see…you're scared.'

'No, I'm not!' Bingyu clenched his fists.

'In my opinion, you're better off leaving,' said Ruoping calmly, 'I'm serious. You can use my car.'

The professor said in confusion:

'Ruoping, are you—'

'Don't worry.' Ruoping stopped Bai and said to Bingyu: 'Just a moment. I'll get the key for you.'

He gave the professor a wink, and left the garage.

It might be better for Bingyu to leave. The irascible playboy fellow was a pain for the investigation. He would definitely get trapped in the rainstorm if he left. In that case, everyone in the house would be safe if it turned out that he was actually the killer.

Ruoping quickly reached the second floor. He turned right and walked to his room, the second room on the right. He'd been away for over four hours.

His backpack was beside the bed. He unzipped it and put his hand into the inner bag.

Empty.

He frowned, and examined the backpack inside out.

The key wasn't there.

He checked his pockets but found nothing. Actually he was pretty sure he'd tucked it into the inner bag of his backpack.

Ruoping began a blanket search of the room. Five minutes later he had given up and went back downstairs.

Back in the garage, Bingyu was leaning against Chengyan's car with his arms crossed over his chest and an unlit cigarette between his lips; Bai and his daughter were standing by the work table, whispering to each other. Tingzhi was leaning against the wall, looking thoughtful; Chengyan was still sitting on the floor, looking distraught.

Bingyu gave Ruoping a disdainful look as he came in.

'My key is missing, too,' announced Ruoping.

'What?' The playboy's cigarette dropped from his lips to the floor.

'I have a hypothesis. Let's prove it,' said Ruoping. He turned to Bai. 'Could you please let me have your car key? I'll explain later.'

'My key? Of course. It's in my study.' The professor walked towards the garage door but stopped abruptly. 'Wait. I think I left it on the work table here.

'Please check.'

'Sure. Give me a minute.' Bai turned to the work table.

'Are you forcing the professor to surrender his car to me?' asked Bingyu, grinning.

'Yes. But you still won't be able to leave.'

'Why not?'

Ruoping didn't answer. Instead, he walked to Chengyan's car and bent down.

'Excuse me,' said Ruoping. 'Could you move a bit? I want to examine this car.'

'What the…' Bingyu cursed and moved aside.

Ruoping quickly examined Chengyan's car, and then the other two cars. Nothing unusual.

Bai turned back from the work table, his face pale.

'I can't find the key.'

'Obviously, all three car keys are missing,' said Ruoping. 'It's easy to guess why.'

Bingyu snarled:

'You're both lying because you don't want me to leave!'

'Be rational,' said Ruoping. 'In that case how do you explain the disappearance of Chengyan's key?'

Bingyu spluttered, but the words failed to form a coherent sentence.

Ruoping said:

'Someone stole all the car keys in order to confine us to the house.'

Bingyu stared. 'That means the killer is going to strike again! I'm doing the smart thing. We should all get out of here as soon as possible!'

'Use your brain. The thief isn't necessarily the killer.'

'Brain, huh?' Bingyu had cooled down a little and, leaning against the wall, took out a new cigarette. 'Then tell me, who is the thief? See? You don't know! You've been fooling me—.'

'I know,' said Ruoping.

'What?' The cigarette dropped from the other's lips again.

Everyone looked at Ruoping with curiosity; even Chengyan raised his head and stared.

'Interesting.' Bingyu crossed his arms across his chest. 'Don't keep us in suspense. Who is this guy?'

'One of the six people here.'

Silence.

'This is my theory,' Ruoping continued. 'It cannot be that all the car keys are just missing by accident. I'm pretty sure I put my key in my backpack in the room, so it's highly unlikely that I dropped it inadvertently. The thefts must have been a planned act, the motive of which, apparently, was to imprison us here. Yet, if that were the case, the best way to achieve that would be to stab the tyres, given that the tools needed are all available in this garage. But no tyre was stabbed.

'The thief chose to steal the keys instead, which was much more difficult because he would need to know where the keys were and carry out three thefts. Let's see who had the chance to do so. There are only two people who know where my room is. One of them is Lingsha, who showed me there after I arrived; the other is someone who happened to meet me on my way to the professor's study last night.'

'But how did the thief know you kept your key in your backpack?' asked Bai.

'He didn't know, but that would be a reasonable guess for him. Where else would I put it?'

'I suppose so.'

'The interesting thing is that this person also chanced to know where you put your car key. Recall that when I came to your study you mentioned you'd left it on the work table here. This person was there with us at that moment.

'The plan was conceived after the thief happened to find out where the professor had left his key. He chose to steal the keys instead of fiddling with the tyres for two reasons. First, theft is convenient for him because he himself owns one of the three keys. Second, he didn't want to damage his own car. Am I correct, Chengyan Fang?'

The thief raised his head slowly to meet Ruoping's eyes, his face expressionless.

16 *(February 11, 2.30 a.m.)*

Bingyu Xu turned off the shower and dried himself.

He left the bathroom, crawled into bed and turned off the light.

What had happened last night was absurd, as if someone had added an unknown colour into the palette to confuse the audience's eyes. It was like a different kind of rainstorm, sweeping everyone in, with no way out.

In the darkness, deeply buried memories swam to the surface.

His old man had been a hopeless drunkard, brought back home almost every midnight by friends; as soon as he was home he would bend over beside the door and begin vomiting.

All he remembered about the old man was his violence. He was beaten every time he got low grades. He'd lived in the shadow of violence until the end of junior high school. Everyday after school he'd dread seeing the old man, who would beat him if he didn't make dinner, didn't do homework—or if he did but didn't do it properly. Things got worse when he tried to hide: then, he'd be almost beaten to death.

His mother never stopped the old man's sadism, partly because she was a victim herself, and partly because she worked at the bar from night to early morning and didn't know what happened during her absence. Very often when he got up in the morning Mom's room was still empty and the old man's snore thundered in another room. The couple didn't sleep in the same room.

He finally realized why he would never feel love from that drunkard: the miserable sod was not even his real father; he was the product of one of his mother's love affairs.

The old man had been killed in a car accident just as his senior high school life was beginning. In one sense, he had caused the drunkard's death. One day, when he'd returned from school and was just getting off his bike, his father, more drunk than ever, had shouted at him: 'Bingyu Xu! You little bastard! You didn't feed my fish this morning!'

The old man kept some guppies and black shrimps, and he was supposed to feed them every morning. He'd forgotten to do so that day and two guppies had died.

Those little creatures might have died for a different reason. For example, the old man seldom changed the water in the aquarium, and a filter was never used. The water always looked murky.

Why should a man immersed in alcoholism and violence care about the death of guppies? He'd never understood.

The old man had grabbed a club and come at him. He'd run away. The old man had stumbled after him, panting, holding the club and a bottle of wine, calling his name.

The next moment he'd heard a big crash and a lot of people screaming. He'd stopped running and turned around.

A truck had stopped at the crossroads and something like a jelly was lying flattened on the ground. What he'd thought was a ball had rolled across the road and come to a halt before him.

There'd been a twisted smile on the old man's face. He'd stood there looking at that smile for a long minute. He'd felt like kicking the head but a policeman had pulled him aside. He'd felt relaxed at that moment, freed from hell.

His mother hadn't shown much sadness. She'd told him to study hard and not to worry about money. After the accident she was away from home more often than before.

School life had been another source of pain. A female transfer student in his class had formed a gang and begun to bully students. He'd been among the victims. That girl's laughter was one of his darkest memories.

He'd finally reported his case to the teacher, who'd called the girl over and questioned her. But she'd fooled the young teacher with clever lies. And he hadn't been doing well in school, which further reduced the teacher's trust in him.

The teacher was a silent young man, paying little attention to his students, burying himself in his laptop all day long. The way he'd looked at female students always struck him as strange. He'd finally given up seeking help from school when he saw the teacher and the girl who had bullied him going to the movies together.

From that day on he'd been forced to learn how to protect himself. He became sensitive to threats and dangers. He became fierce and defensive. Nowadays, when darkness fell, some recurrent images just kept haunting him: the old man's head, the female transfer student, and the silent teacher.

The first time he'd seen Yunxin Liu he'd known instantly that she'd be a thorn in his side. She was the spitting image of the transfer student....

He left his room and knocked on the adjacent door.
'Who is it?'
'It's me, Bingyu Xu. Do you have a minute?'
'What's the matter?'
'Let me in and I'll tell you.'
There was a pause. Then the door opened to reveal Chengyan, who left it open and went back to sit on the wicker chair in the corner of the room. The only light came from a bedside lamp.
Bingyu went in and sat down on the edge of the bed.
He took a cigarette out and lit it.
'Smoke?' he offered.
'You know I don't.'
'You should try. It helps at times like these.' He smiled. 'I'm not trying to force you.'
'What do you want?' Chengyan's deadpan expression didn't change.
'I'm just dropping by.'
'Dropping by?' The look in Chengyan's eyes hardened suddenly. 'Don't make fun of me. Get out!'
'Easy, man. I know you're in a bad mood. Your girl was killed, you became a suspect, and you're confined to this place.'
'I didn't become a suspect.'
'Well, you stole the car keys in order to be with your girl for a longer period of time.'
'I never said that!'
'You didn't, but everyone knows it. Ruoping Lin asked you whether you'd done it so as to get more time to be with someone, and your face betrayed you. Ironically, the girl's dead now.'
'I didn't kill her.'
'Love and hatred can be the same thing.'
'Get out of here!' Chengyan clenched his fists.
Bingyu sprang to his feet and lunged at him, grabbing him by the neck and pinning him to the wall. They glared at each other angrily before he let the other fall to the floor, clutching his neck and coughing painfully.

'Listen to me.' Bingyu took the cigarette out of his lips and looked at the ceiling. 'I'm here to seek your cooperation. We have a common enemy.'

Chengyan was still coughing.

'Or maybe I should say she's our friend, because she can bring us joy.' He returned to the bed and sat down again.

'I think Yunxin killed Xiangya. She's the only one with a motive. She was a sadist, can't you see that? That's why Xiangya had that scar! I don't know how she committed that fancy murder, but this pretty much matches her style. It's got to be her.' He threw the cigarette on the floor. 'Hey, say something. I know you've been itching to kill that madwoman!'

The other remained silent.

'I don't like her, either. And now I have a plan.' He got up again, bent down beside Chengyan and whispered: 'This house is cursed. A lot of people have died here, and I have a hunch that more are going to die soon. There's a rainstorm and we're stuck here. We might all die…it's like the end of the world. Why not do something we've been wanting to do before we perish?'

Chengyan raised his head and looked at him with vacant eyes.

'Let's take revenge on that bitch,' continued Bingyu with a grin. 'I've a feeling you know what I mean.'

After a long pause, Chengyan muttered something under his breath while staring hard at the suitcase under the bed, from which the cover of a DVD was poking out.

The title could be seen clearly: it was *Cave of Death*.

17 *(February 11, 3.30 a.m.)*

It was three-thirty in the morning. The House of Rain was like an abandoned castle.

Ruoping stood in the middle of the crime scene, contemplating.

A couple of minutes ago he'd unlocked the double-doors and come into the murder room again.

Someone was dead. More people might die. The only way to save everyone was to solve the case.

He studied the objects in the room again: an empty clothes stand, a saw, and a fishing line circling the base of the stand.

One end of the line appeared to have been torn rather than cut. Perhaps these objects together somehow formed a death trap, but that still didn't explain how the head of the victim had disappeared.

Another question was why the head had also been torn off, not cut off. So then why was the saw stained with blood? A closer examination revealed that the blood-stained area was not on the teeth of the saw, but on the surface. It looked as though blood had splashed on it when Xiangya Yue's head had been ripped off, not that it had been used as the murder weapon itself.

The body lay with the neck almost touching the door.

The room was much smaller than a normal guest room, and apparently not intended for that purpose at all.

Holding a handkerchief to avoid fingerprints, Ruoping examined the body and the objects in the room yet again. He was gradually becoming certain of two things.

First, the victim was undoubtedly Xiangya Yue. She was the only one missing from the house, and the size of the body matched hers. Second, the fishing line, the clothes stand and the saw were all covered by a thick layer of dust, which meant that they hadn't been used for quite some time. Therefore, they couldn't have served as a death trap. In which case, what was their purpose? It was baffling.

He felt dizzy again. Each time he was in this room he felt dizzy. The loud sounds of heavy rain made his mind wander.

There was an evil and dark force in this house, spreading terror. Ruoping didn't believe in supernatural powers, but this impossible murder defied comprehension.

He tucked the handkerchief into his pocket and left the room. As he closed the door, he pressed a round button adjacent to it in order to turn the light off, and left.

As Ruoping was about to walk through the double-doors, the noise of the rain outside diminished, and he was able to detect the sound of footsteps behind him.

He stopped, turned around slowly, and looked down the dark stairwell.

He tiptoed towards the stairs and pressed the light button on the wall.

As the darkness dispersed he caught a glimpse of someone turning round and rushing back downstairs. In that brief moment Ruoping could see that the fleeing figure was a man, but couldn't see who it was.

He quickly followed the man downstairs, but lost sight of him. As he reached the first floor, he could hear more quick footsteps from below and kept heading down using the handrail to guide him.

When he was within a few steps of the bottom, he could hear the sound of door being unbolted and saw a beam of light stabbing the darkness.

The man escaped onto the central corridor of the ground floor and disappeared.

As Ruoping rushed towards the double-doors he stumbled over something, but managed to steady himself.

He stepped back, fumbling around for the light button on the wall.

As the light dispelled the darkness, Ruoping froze.

Lying on the floor, in a pool of dried blood, was an object shaped like a battered cauliflower. A twisted face covered with messy hair stared up at him. Although it was difficult to recognise, it had to be Xiangya.

He took a deep breath and decided to leave the head there for the time being.

As he hurried into the central corridor, there was no sign of the man he'd been chasing. He checked the dining room and the recreation room, but found nothing there, either.

Who was the man and what had he been doing on the stairs?

Judging from the direction from which he'd been coming, he'd probably intended to visit the crime scene. The killer always returns to the scene of the crime....

Ruoping returned to the central corridor. As he approached the intersection of corridors, he heard someone cursing.

'Damn! It's locked.'

It was Bingyu's voice.

He stopped and peered ahead. Bingyu and Chengyan were standing by the door to the left of the north staircase.

'Be quiet,' said the latter. 'The maidservants' rooms are nearby.'

'What do we do now? I've knocked three times but there's no answer. Is she trying to make fools of us?'

'Turn off the light to force her come out,' said Chengyan. 'Let me try.'

So saying, he pressed the button on the wall nearest the doorknob. The light didn't seem to be working.

'It doesn't work!' cried Bingyu, giving the door a hard kick.

'What are you doing? You'll wake everyone up!' said his companion, looking tense and taut.

'Maybe she's already dead,' grinned Bingyu. 'The room wasn't locked when I passed by earlier. But now it is. Obviously she's inside. Perhaps she left from the other door in the room. That door leads to the tennis court outside the house. But I'm willing to bet she's still inside!' He kicked the door again.

Ruoping stepped forward.

'Do you need the hatchet?' he asked in an expressionless voice.

18 *(February 11, 3.50 a.m.)*

Yunxin Liu wasn't afraid of the dark, but she was afraid of people who create darkness. And she could feel that some part of her echoed with darkness.

She was not particularly brave, but would fight hard out of self-preservation. She was selfish, but who wasn't?

Descending the northern staircase, she pulled her scarf tighter.

The red scarf was one of her favourite decorations. Red represents desire and rebellion. Together with the carefully chosen dress and shoes, the scarf presented her in the best light.

Xiangya's death had been a great shock to her. Although she'd hated Xiangya, she'd never expected she would die this way.

She thought of her older sister, Jie, who was arrogant, calculating and narrow-minded. She had all the same characteristics as her sister. Their parents had separated ten years ago. Dad had committed suicide on the railway lines; Mom had gone to jail for theft, and was housed by Yunxin's uncle after her imprisonment because Jie had refused to take care of her. Yunxin had lived with Jie thereafter.

In her high school days, she'd been constantly bullied. She would sob out her troubles to Jie, who would hold her softly by the shoulders and comfort her with the wisdom of survival.

'Be a bad girl,' said Jie. 'For women, control their weaknesses. For men, never give them your heart; use them for your own purposes.' She had kept the words in mind.

Yunxin hated girls more beautiful than she was. She had an urge to destroy them as soon as she saw them. She'd had that urge when she'd first seen Xiangya, who was not only more beautiful, but also more popular and talented, than she was.

In order to destroy that beautiful doll, she'd set Xiangya up; she'd used a stupid man to fool Xiangya and then controlled her weakness. She'd put Jie's wisdom into practice.

But now joy had gone, and fear had come in its place.

She reached the ground floor. At the far end of the central corridor was the hallway; the maidservant's rooms were to her right, the laundry and the stockroom to her left.

The empty corridor chilled her bones. How could she have the courage to walk there alone after someone had been murdered? She knew the answer perfectly. But maybe she didn't fully understand herself.

What had happened not long ago came to mind....

As she'd been about to crawl into bed, someone had knocked at the door.

'It's me, Chengyan.'

She'd got out of bed. She'd been in her nightgown but she didn't mind.

Chengyan's face had appeared at the door. He'd handed her a note, then turned and disappeared into the darkness.

Yunxin had closed the door, her heart beating fast and her cheeks feeling warm. She'd opened the folded note.

Dear Yunxin,

Don't be surprised by what I'm about to say. It would only be a matter of time before you found out.

Everyone thinks I'm crazy about Xiangya and I hate you, because you've enslaved her. That was true before, but not any longer.

Xiangya's death was a great shock. But after the grief, something buried deep in my heart began to reveal itself, and I was even more shocked to learn what it was....

You won't believe me, but this is the truth. The one I've been crazy about is not Xiangya, but you.

No, I'm not kidding. It's easy to explain. I'd been jealous of Xiangya, because she enjoyed your company all along; I pretended to hate you because I didn't have enough courage to accept the truth. My attitude towards Xiangya was only a disguise.

Xiangya's ugly mutilated body meant a new start. Things are different now.

We're isolated from the outer world, and this place could be where we rest in peace. Both of us may not have a second chance to speak our mind to each other. If you'd like to, meet me later at four in the room next to the north staircase (on your right when you face the hallway). Please close the door after you go in. I'll knock three times, and don't open the door till then.

Do come.

89

She'd folded the note with trembling hands.

Why had she been concealing her affection? Why had she been pretending to be his enemy? Because she could never give her heart to anyone, and because she had trained herself to be heartless.

Why not just fall from virtue at this rainy night, before death took their lives away?

Yunxin arrived early. She pressed the light button, opened the door, and went in.

The oblong room was roughly one third of the size of a normal guest room, having two doors facing each other. Lingsha had told them that the back door led to the tennis court outside, which was no longer in use. The room had been intended as a changing room for tennis games, so there were hangers on the wall. There was nothing else in the room.

The back door was closed, which reminded her that she should close and lock the front door in case anyone accidentally came in.

She turned the lock, but the bolt failed to move exactly into the hole on the doorframe; she had to press the door hard with her hand for the bolt to fit snugly.

As she turned round, it occurred to her to take a look at the tennis court. She used to play tennis.

Yunxin went over to the back door and unlocked it.

But the door wouldn't move as she tried to pull it. It got stuck. The person who'd made the doors of this room hadn't done a good job. Maybe that was why people no longer used the tennis court.

Applying more effort, she finally managed to open the door. The wind came in.

She felt better now. She'd felt dizzy as she'd entered this room, probably because it had been long abandoned and become very stuffy.

The rain had stopped outside. The light from the room was too weak for her to see anything clearly in the court.

She closed the door but it got stuck again. She began to feel impatient, so she used her full strength to move it.

The loud bang sounded in the quiet night as the door moved into the right position.

She became nervous. The sound might have woken the maidservants. She shouldn't have been so impatient.

90

Yunxin turned around and listened carefully. It occurred to her that she should turn the light off in case anyone noticed she was in the room.

As she was trying the buttons at waist-level on the wall, a strong force suddenly pulled her from behind and her scarf tightened.

She clutched the scarf quickly, but it kept tightening....

W—what was happening...? She realised the answer right away.

Someone must have opened the back door and attacked her from behind. She'd forgotten to lock the back door after closing it!

It must be the murderer who killed Xiangya!

She struggled to break free but failed. Her enemy was too powerful.

Terribly powerful....

As she struggled, three knocks sounded on the front door.

It was Chengyan!

She fought the unknown killer with all of her strength. Help was only a few steps away. Chengyan was waiting for her behind the other door. As long as she could fight back, her life could be saved....

She couldn't die now!

For a moment she thought she would make it, but she soon realised it was impossible. Death had won.

As she lost consciousness someone cursed outside:

'Damn! It's locked!'

It was not Chengyan. It was Bingyu.

Her last strength was gone. Darkness fell.

Chapter 3
Footprints of the Ghost

19 *(February 11, 4.15 a.m.)*

A crack appeared in the door of the changing room. Ruoping had avoided hacking at the lock. This was another door without a keyhole.

Panting, he put down the hatchet.

Chengyan and Bingyu stood nearby, the former appearing worried and the latter relaxed.

The two maidservants looked on with terror in their eyes.

The crack was now big enough for him to put his hand through and unlock the door. The bolt didn't move easily until he applied more strength.

Finally, the door opened outwards.

The maidservants screamed and turned away quickly. The others took a deep breath.

'Again.' Bingyu took out a cigarette packet and fiddled with it.

Chengyan stared intently at what was inside.

Ruoping turned to Ru. 'Could you please report this to the professor and ask him to assemble everyone in the living room? And please get me the camera in the study. Thank you.'

Panic-stricken, Ru nodded and left hurriedly.

Ruoping stepped into the room and examined the body.

Yunxin Liu lay on her back with her head up and her face twisted, clutching at the red scarf around her neck. Apparently her neck was broken for it was at an impossible angle, wedged against the back door so that her chin was buried deep into her chest.

'Strangled to death,' said Ruoping, squatting down in front of the body. 'The scarf was the murder weapon.'

One end of the scarf dangled from her neck and touched the floor. It appeared tattered and torn.

After a moment's scrutiny, Ruoping stood up.

'What happened?' Renze Bai's voice came from behind.

'Another victim,' said Ruoping.

On seeing Yunxin's body the professor turned his head quickly away. 'The others are all in the living room. I'll see you there'.

'I'll be there as soon as I can.'

Bai handed Ruoping the black camera.

Ruoping was soon left alone. He took some photos of the body.

After a second check of the body, he wrapped his hand with his handkerchief and tried to open the door to the tennis court.

At first the door refused to move but it eventually surrendered. As the door suddenly flew open, Yunxin's head and shoulders hit the muddy ground outside the room.

A cold wind blew in. It was pitch dark outside.

The rain had stopped at some point before four, but might well start again soon.

He noticed a small piece of red material on the ground beside the door.

He bent down and picked it up. It was part of Yunxin's scarf.

He wrapped it in his handkerchief and tucked it into his pocket.

Something caught Ruoping's eye. A couple of red threads had got caught on the doorframe at waist level.

Ruoping pondered for a moment, then took hold of Yunxin's legs and pulled until her head was completely inside the room.

He closed the back door after several failed attempts, locked it and left the room.

There was a killing machine in this house, coldblooded and ruthless. Who was he? Why did he kill?

He'd noticed something wrong with the murder that had just taken place. Further investigation would be needed, but he was afraid that the result would make the whole thing even more nightmarish.

Ruoping went to the living room. There was a frightened audience awaiting him.

'Bad news,' said Ruoping. 'Murder again.'

There was no need to say who the victim was. It could only be the one who was absent.

Ruoping observed their reactions closely. The killer was almost certainly one of them, and a perfect actor.

'I know all of you are still in shock, but we're in a race with time if we want to prevent a third murder.' He pulled a chair and sat down.

'Ruoping is right,' said Bai in a weak voice. 'The only way to stop all this insanity is to ferret out the killer.'

The clock in the living room pointed to four-forty. Everyone's sleepiness had been chased away by terror.

Ruoping said:

'I examined the body and found that Yunxin had expired just as we were breaking in. The time of death was probably around four o'clock.'

'In that case, neither Chengyan nor I can be the killer,' said Bingyu, fidgeting with his lighter.

'You're right. By the way, why were you there?'

'Am I obliged to answer?'

'If you don't want to become a public enemy.'

'I suggest you be cooperative,' said Bai.

'Ask Chengyan,' mumbled Bingyu.

Chengyan looked up and sighed. 'We made an appointment with Yunxin.'

'For what?'

'Xiangya.'

'Explain.'

Bingyu hesitated. 'We think Yunxin had a motive in Xiangya's case. We wanted to do some investigation.'

'Why in that room?'

'It's not relevant to the case. We just needed a private space and that room is never locked.'

'All right. Did you tell her to meet you at four?'

'Yes.'

'Did you tell her to lock the door?'

'We just told her to close the door.'

'I want to ask Cindy and Ru some questions,' Ruoping turned to the maidservants. 'Did you notice anything unusual before or after four o'clock?'

The two maidservants looked at each other. Ru responded: 'I—I saw Miss Yunxin entering the changing room.'

'Please elaborate.'

'I woke up some minutes before four because of a nightmare. The rain had already stopped by then. The room was a bit stuffy, so I went out into the corridor and opened the windows opposite my room. At that moment I heard footsteps from the north staircase. As I went back to my room I caught a glimpse of someone...it was Miss Yunxin.'

'Are you absolutely sure it was she?'

'What I'm absolutely sure of was her dress....'

'I see. Please continue.'

95

'Since I was curious about what she was doing, I stood by the door and listened attentively. Then there was a loud bang.'

'What kind of bang?'

'Like someone slamming a door.'

Ruoping took out his notepad and wrote down what Ru had said.

'And then?'

'Cindy was awakened by the loud noise. I told her what had happened. Then we heard people approaching. It was Mr. Bingyu and Mr. Chengyan. That's all I know.'

'Last question. Did anyone come out of the room after Yunxin went in?'

'No. It was impossible. I was watching the room.'

Bai straightened himself up in the sofa.

Ruoping asked him: 'Regarding the changing room, do you know that there's something wrong with both doors?'

'I do. My brother complained to me about that. He suspected that Shengfeng Shi deliberately left architectural defects like that in the house out of spite. But that was just his guess.'

'That's why the tennis court and changing room were no longer in use?'

'Yes. Another reason was that the family seldom had a chance to get together and play.'

'The back door is supposed to be always locked, isn't it?'

'Yes.'

'Are you sure it was locked today?'

'Why not?'

Ruoping looked at the maidservants for the answer. Ru said: 'I don't know. We've just moved in, and there are so many rooms that we haven't had time to clean....'

'It's all right. Now let's get to another matter.' Ruoping surveyed everyone. 'Alibis. I want to know what you were doing at four o'clock.'

'Most people were asleep at that time,' said Bingyu in his usual disdainful tone. 'You're just wasting time.'

'I still need to know. Just tell me.'

The investigation was soon over. Just as Bingyu had said, Lingsha and Tingzhi were in their room when Ru and the professor had woken them up, which meant no one had an alibi.

Chengyan and Bingyu didn't seem to have had the chance to commit the crime. Moreover, if Ru wasn't lying, then she and Cindy were also innocent.

Everyone was looking tired. Ruoping closed his notepad and said: 'There is one last thing I want to confirm. It's about how the killer got in and out of the changing room. According to Ru, no one left the room after Yunxin went in. So the killer must have left the room by the back door.

'The back door was not locked when we broke in, which supports the hypothesis that the killer left that way. In that case, he must have left footprints on the tennis court. I wasn't able to check the footprints because it was too dark outside.'

Ruoping stopped and there was a moment of silence.

'Now, everyone please show me the soles of your shoes.'

There was no dirt at all on the soles of anyone's shoes.

'Is anyone wearing a different pair of shoes from yesterday?' asked Ruoping.

Again, the answer was negative.

'I don't think the killer is that stupid,' said Tingzhi. 'He might have used spare shoes in the hallway or cleaned his own after the murder.'

'Or he didn't wear shoes at all,' sneered Bingyu.

'We'll know after we check the footprints.'

'I have a question,' said Bai. 'If the killer left the changing room by the back door, how did he get back into the house?'

'What are the options?'

'There are only three doors, all on the south side of the house: the front door, the door to the badminton hall, and the door to the garage.'

'I suppose all three doors are locked from the inside?'

'Of course. Technically, the garage door is electronically controlled.'

'He could've re-entered the house from that door if he'd had the remote control.' Ruoping stood up. 'We'd better check the footprints now. Is the tennis court equipped with lighting, professor?'

'Yes.'

'Could you turn it on?'

The professor stood up. 'Of course. The switch is in the servants' living room. Let's go.'

'Let's go together, all of us,' said Ruoping.

They left the living room and walked towards the north staircase. No one spoke and the only sounds were their footsteps.

The door of the changing room was half closed; the light was still on. Ruoping signalled everyone to wait in front of the staircase while Bai went to turn on the tennis court lights.

Ruoping entered the changing room and closed the door behind him.

Yunxin's body was still there, staring at the ceiling.

He averted his eyes, walked to the back door and opened it.

It was pitch-dark outside. Suddenly, darkness was dispelled.

The tennis court was connected to the north wall of the house, surrounded by three sides of green wire. There were lights set on the west and east side of the court.

Ruoping stood frozen.

The ground of the red clay court was completely intact, with not a mark on the surface.

20 *(February 11, 6.00 a.m.)*

Tingzhi Yan sank into the sofa in the living room and observed all the exhausted people.

Ruoping, Bai and the maidservants were out in the corridor, looking for any trace of footprints. The rest remained in the room with her, taking a nap.

Tingzhi also felt tired but she needed to stay awake. She tried to focus her mind on the case.

A smart and confident girl, she liked intellectual games such as solving unsolved cases, paranormal activities, and science questions. She could spend a whole day wrestling with such puzzles. Her mother had been worried that she wouldn't be able to get a boyfriend because she wasn't interested in men. But her mother was wrong; it was only men who didn't use their brains who didn't interest her.

Tingzhi didn't like to collaborate with people; she preferred to work independently. She never sought help or advice, and would never share any theory with others unless she could prove it was true.

She had come here to solve a puzzle, but hadn't found any clues so far. She was not sure whether the present murders were relevant to her investigation; she couldn't find any strong connections.

Footsteps coming from the corridor interrupted her thoughts. Ruoping and Bai appeared at the entrance of the living room.

As soon as Tingzhi saw their faces, she knew the investigation had yielded no results.

'The maidservants are preparing breakfast,' Bai announced wearily. 'The food will be ready soon.'

A moment later everyone was in the dining room. On the dining table were two plates of Chinese bread and another two of steamed buns. Each person was served a bowl of soybean milk.

The meal looked delicious but apparently no one had any appetite for it.

Tingzhi quickly finished eating.

As she was about to leave the dining room, Ruoping's voice came from behind.

'You'd better not act alone.'

'Don't worry about me. I'll be fine.'

Tingzhi left.

Walking along the corridor northwards, Tingzhi soon reached the intersection. To the right lay the piano room and, if one continued walking southwards, the badminton court. She played neither, so she turned left.

At the end of the corridor was the movie room. Tingzhi pressed the light button for the room, went in, and closed the door behind her.

There was a purple-curtained window opposite the door; a sofa stood against the south wall; a black table was placed in front of the sofa.

There were two large bookcases with glass doors in front of the east and west walls, holding countless DVDs, most of which didn't interest Tingzhi.

A projector hung from the ceiling, facing the screen on the north wall. There were speakers below the screen. There was also photographic equipment stacked in the corner.

The quietness of the room created an air of chill.

Tingzhi was not in the mood to watch movies, so she decided to leave.

As her hand touched the doorknob, something in one of the bookcases caught her attention.

Through the glass doors of the bookcase she saw some English-learning material among the movie DVDs on the bottom shelf. Such material was common in bookstores: the textbook and CD were packaged together in a plastic box. Seven boxes in total were stacked inside.

Tingzhi bent down and opened the doors. She took out a box entitled 'Common sentence patterns in English.'

It struck her as odd that learning material had been put there, mixed in with entertainment DVDs. The room was for watching movies, not for learning English.

She opened the box.

There were four digital videotapes inside, each with a sticker on it showing a date.

She opened another box. The same contents. It turned out that the seven boxes held twenty-eight DV tapes in total. The dates showed that they had been recorded in three different time periods: last February, the February of the year before that, and between July and mid-September of that year.

What was all this about? If she could play these DV tapes....

She put down the box and went over to the north side of the room, where she could see a camera in the corner. It was in working order.

Tingzhi went back to the bookcase with the camera, selected the tape recorded in early July the year before last and placed it in the camera.

She turned off the light. Darkness made her mind more focused. She held the camera with both hands and watched.

The first scene was a corridor, at the end of which was a set of double-doors. At first she thought the person making the recording was standing in the second floor corridor with his or her back facing the study. But she soon realised that the corridor was not quite the same as she remembered it.

The person turned left onto a narrow corridor along which two rooms stood side by side.

The scene suddenly turned to a door in the distance.

No. This was not the second floor....

The room would be Lingsha's room if the recorder were on the second floor. Furthermore, the colour and decoration of the door were different.

The person recording moved again. He or she walked towards the double-doors, opened them, turned right, walked towards the end of the corridor, and turned right again. He or she reached a balcony. The camera shot moved downwards and the badminton court appeared in view.

Now she was absolutely sure. The individual was on the first floor; it followed that the room she had just seen was that of Lingsha's cousin—Yuyun.

The tape had been recorded the year before last, when Yuyun was still alive.

A chill ran down her spine.

The camera started roaming randomly....

Tingzhi removed the tape and replaced it with another recorded in the following month.

She played four more.

The contents were almost the same, all random shots of the house. Sometimes the person recording went out of the house, but most of the time he or she remained inside, roaming around aimlessly.

They never spoke or appeared in any of the shots. There were no other people, either.

The DV tapes had been recorded either in February, July, August or September....

Wait, weren't these winter and summer vacations?

A thought crossed her mind. She decided to watch the tapes in order.

She played the earliest tape: the first of February of the year before last.

The first scene was the dining room. There was food on the table... Next, the view switched to the corridor, where someone was making his way slowly towards the double-doors at the end, leading to the hallway.

It was an old man, bald and in a wheelchair, with his back to the camera.

The recorder followed him at a distance. There was something sinister about the banal scene.

The old man stopped before reaching the end of the corridor and pivoted to his right to face another set of double-doors leading to the south staircase.

They were open and the wheelchair passed through....

What happened next came as a stunning shock. Tingzhi sat frozen, her mind exploding.

At first, it seemed to be incredible, inconceivable... but gradually it became entirely plausible!

She remained seated, thinking back about the two impossible murders. Now she knew. She knew how the impossibility had been achieved!

Although she now knew the trick, there was still no clue as to the identity of the killer.

Was he or she also responsible for the murders last year?

She felt she was close to the truth. But before the truth came to light she couldn't let anyone know that she held the key to the impossible crimes; otherwise she would be in extreme danger.

As she thought about watching the rest of the DV tapes, a disturbing thought crossed her mind: did the killer know this tape contained the secret of the magic? If so, she shouldn't stay here for too long....

All of a sudden the doorknob turned and the door opened slightly.

A figure appeared in the doorway.

21 *(February 11, 6.30 a.m.)*

Breakfast in the dining room took place in complete silence.

Ruoping's investigation had turned out to be in vain. No shoes had been stolen, no footprints had been found anywhere on the ground floor, and no locks had been broken.

The most baffling thing was that there were no footprints outside the house, either. Not even one on the way from the tennis court to the garage—the assumed escape route for the killer. The conclusion was that no one had gone between the tennis court and the garage; otherwise the person must have had wings.

Other evidence also proved the hypothesis about the escape route to be untenable. Aside from the back door of the changing room, the only entrance to the tennis court—on the northwest side of the court— was padlocked. The padlock was intact, and the key had already been lost before Jingfu Bai died. Even if the killer could have travelled from the garage to the tennis court without leaving any footprints, he would have needed to climb over the wire cage, fly over the court, open a formidable door, and strangle Yunxin, without leaving any traces during this long process. It was utterly impossible.

As Ruoping and Bai were doing the search with the help of the maidservants, the others had stayed behind in the living room and slept, because no one dared to be alone. Some lay on the sofa, some on the floor, all were exhausted. When Ruoping and the others returned to the living room it was already several minutes past six.

Cindy and Ru set about preparing breakfast. Ruoping and Bai woke everyone up at six-thirty.

During breakfast everyone remained silent. Even Bingyu kept his mouth shut.

Bingyu and Chengyan finished their food and left. Now only Ruoping, Bai and his daughter remained in the room.

'You must be tired,' said the professor. 'This case is like the devil's joke.'

'Do you believe in the devil?' asked Ruoping.

Bai pushed his dish aside and said: 'I don't believe in the religious devil, but I do believe that many things cannot be explained by science.'

'Maybe they will be in the future. Science just needs to make more progress.'

'In that case, we can't, by definition, know the answer now. This case could be a perfect example.'

'I don't think so.'

'You're a detective. You believe that logic and science can explain everything. But people my age have doubts about that.'

'I understand what you mean, but I still think the two deaths in this house are the product of someone's malice aforethought.'

'I doubt we can come up with any reasonable explanation.'

'I've solved seemingly impossible cases before. In every case there was eventually a rational explanation. I believe it's so with this case. Now, I have some thoughts about the second murder. Let's brainstorm, if both of you are interested.'

The professor and his daughter nodded in unison.

Cindy had cleared away all the dishes and cups. The neat and tidy table reminded Ruoping of the tennis court.

'Since the evidence shows that the killer couldn't have accessed the changing room by the back door, the only possibility is the front door.'

'But we've excluded that possibility, too,' said Bai.

'True. Even if the killer managed to escape without the maidservant noticing, there was still a problem: he or she had to lock the door from the outside. Perhaps the killer used a trick to do that, but it's hard to imagine it could have been done without being seen by the maidservants watching nearby. Moreover, don't forget there is a problem with the lock. I doubt the standard wire or thread trick would work.'

'There's a third possibility,' began Lingsha. 'The killer never entered the room.'

'You mean there was a death trap in the room?'

'Yes. We discussed that already in the first case.'

'An interesting theory. But I can't see how.'

'Come to think of it, another question we asked in the first case is equally applicable in the second: why did the killer bother to create the impossible situation?' said Bai.

'Good point. What complicates matters is another factor present in both cases: the unpredictable movements of the victims.'

'What do you mean?' asked Bai.

'In both cases, the victims went to the rooms in which they both later died, unexpectedly. It seems impossible for the killer to have known with certainty that Xiangya would enter the room where she was killed. Likewise it seems impossible for the killer to be sure that Yunxin would make an appointment with Chengyan in the changing room. In both cases, how could the killer know where the victims would go, so he could set up the murder trick *in advance* in the room, assuming the trick required prior setup?'

'That's a point. I never thought of that. The killer seems prescient.' Bai pondered for a moment and continued: 'So Chengyan was probably the killer. He made appointments with both victims. Perhaps he gave Xiangya some hints about which room to go to....'

'He's certainly the most suspicious. And he just so happened to be on the crime scene already in both cases. But I can't work out how he could have accomplished the murders.'

The discussion ended. The professor seemed to have something to discuss with his daughter, so Ruoping left them alone.

He stepped into the corridor, turned left, and went to the living room. Chengyan and Bingyu were playing cards. He took a seat next to them.

'Do you want to join in?' asked Chengyan. 'I know this is supposedly not the right moment to play this, but what else can we do?'

'If you don't mind.'

They began playing Sevens.

Ruoping looked at the bad hand he'd been dealt and said: 'I don't mean to be insensitive, but how do you feel now that two of your friends have died?'

'I don't know,' said Chengyan, looking at his cards. 'Humans are strange animals. Sometimes they don't know what they're thinking about, and they fail to interpret their emotions and reactions.'

'Sounds deep.'

'What I said is a good proof of it—I don't know what I'm saying.'

Bingyu snorted and showed signs of impatience.

After they'd been playing for a while in silence, Ruoping began again.

'Did you love Xiangya?' He played the nine of spades.

'Stupid question,' sneered Bingyu.

Chengyan didn't answer until the playboy had finished his round.

'I realised that the one I loved was the imaginary Xiangya, not the real one. When I saw her body, I saw ugliness, not only in her, but also in me.'

'You act rather than think, like the main character in *Cave of Death*.'

Chengyan smiled. 'What I did was an uninteresting theft. It's no match for your love of solving the case. I found my love blind and ugly. It wasn't love at all.'

Ruoping played the ten of spades. 'Why did Xiangya run out of the library?'

'You like asking questions, don't you?'

'Answers matter more for me.'

Chengyan threw down a jack. 'She escaped because she was afraid.'

'Afraid of what?'

'Of... me.'

'You?'

'Of what I might do to her. Like what I might have done to Yunxin.' He stopped abruptly.

After a pause, Ruoping played his last card.

'I think it had something to do with red wine.'

'You win the game.'

Ruoping had been dealt a bad hand but he'd still won. He needed the same luck with this case. He stood up.

'That was fun. Now I must go.'

He left the living room and turned right. Bai and his daughter had gone. The maidservants were in the dining room, eating breakfast. They both looked tired.

He continued northwards until he reached the changing room, where he stood in front of the door, meditating, like a philosopher.

After a moment he moved his stiff legs. There was pain but no gain.

Ruoping returned to the intersection and turned right.

At the end of the corridor was the movie room. Out of curiosity, he decided to have a look.

He put his hand on the doorknob and opened the door....

22 *(February 11, 7.45 a.m.)*

Tingzhi put the camera behind her and turned to the figure in the doorway. It was Ruoping.

'Sorry. I didn't know you were here.'

'Never mind. I was just about to leave.'

'I didn't mean to disturb you. I was just looking around. Excuse me.' He closed the door.

The room was silent again.

Now what should she do?

Finishing watching the DV tapes was not a good idea. It was not safe staying here alone. She should put away the tapes and leave. But wait, shouldn't she tell the detective—Ruoping Lin—about the tapes?

On second thoughts, she decided not to do so, for three reasons. First, she didn't like to share her findings with others. Second, the present case might be related to last year's case, which she was investigating, and didn't want anyone to know. The third reason, and the most important one, was that she'd rather not trust anyone at the moment, including Ruoping Lin.

Tingzhi decided to take with her the last tape she had watched. It would play an important role in her plan. She would come back here at some point to finish watching the remaining ones.

After putting away the tapes, she left the room. There was no one in the corridor. There were sounds of people playing coming from the table tennis room. Ruoping was probably playing inside and waiting for her to leave.

Tingzhi walked slowly to the intersection of the corridors, thinking about her plan. If she used that tape to trap the killer....

She thought about verifying the locked room trick, but decided to go back to her room first.

As she was about to turn north, she saw Ruoping going into the living room.

She was surprised. Hadn't he been in the table tennis room?

Then who was it she'd heard playing...?

23 *(February 11, 8.00 a.m.)*

Ruoping sat alone on the sofa, meditating again.

He reassessed Yunxin's case. The most reasonable guess would be that the killer never entered the changing room. In that case, there must be some sort of powerful death trap that could break a person's neck.

Suppose this hard-to-imagine theory was true, it seemed that the force could only have come from the door leading to the outside....

Wait!

A thought suddenly struck him.

Suppose the death trap had come from the sky....

Yunxin had opened the back door and put her head outside; at that moment the death trap had dropped from above and grabbed her neck. In other words, the killer might have manipulated the apparatus through the window of the room directly above the changing room.

But there was still one problem: how did the killer close the back door from above?

Ruoping decided to check the plausibility of his theory. If it was workable he might find more clues.

He left the living room in a hurry.

Two minutes later he was in the garage. He grabbed a raincoat hanging on the wall, opened the electronic roll-up door, and walked out.

It was raining again. His shoes were soon wet.

Ruoping walked northwards along the west side of the house. He'd chosen that route because he hadn't wanted to see Yunxin's body again. Eventually he reached the north side of the house and stood beside the tennis court, from which point he could see the back door of the changing room through the wire cage.

He looked up.

The part of the wall above the changing room door was perfectly smooth and clean.

There was no window at all there.

24 *(Zhengyu Jiang's Soliloquy)*

I'm sitting on the bed.

My mind is confused.

Earlier during the card game in the living room Chengyan had been talking about the obsession brought about by love.

Chengyan had taken action; he'd organised that crazy theft. All he'd wanted was more time with Xiangya.

The rainstorm had isolated the house. The isolation had made him feel different, invoking something deep inside him.

I'd been fretful since I'd learnt what Chengyan had done. Eventually I'd gone to the table tennis room and hit the ball against the wall. Table tennis is my favourite sport and it made me feel relaxed.

I've become obsessed with Tingzhi.

Tingzhi is a work of art and I am a connoisseur. But I've been thinking about becoming a collector.

I've been hesitant to make such a move, because it goes against my principle: the principle of being an onlooker, of not getting involved. I used to be a shadow whose presence was overlooked by everyone. But now I'm a transcendental being, ubiquitous and omniscient. It hasn't been easy to achieve this state but I've made it. Stepping into these miserable people's world could mark the end of my transcendence. Should I risk it?

Indeed, Chengyan's determination had moved me.

In this isolated house in which two murders have already taken place, I can foresee more deaths. Despair is already everywhere. Even though I know that all this has nothing to do with me, I can't be certain that I would be absolutely free from danger.

One should grasp the last chance before the end of the world, and that was exactly what Chengyan had done.

A part of my mind has begun to crack. A voice inside has clamoured for adventure.

The crack is widening....

I don't remember how long I've been fighting this inner revolution, but finally I've surrendered. I smile, because at long last I've made a hard decision. I should have done it earlier.

I am no longer a connoisseur.

I am a collector now, and I have a plan.

In my mind's eye, I can see Tingzhi asleep, probably having a sweet dream.

My own dream will come true soon enough....

25 *(February 11, 12.30 p.m.)*

Ruoping spent the whole morning examining all the doors and windows on the ground floor and finding nothing unusual. There was no evidence to show there had been an intruder.

After lunch, it occurred to him that Xiangya's head was still in the south staircase. He didn't want to move it before the police came. But he felt that he should cover the miserable thing with something.

He went to the living room and searched for anything that could do the job. He bent down to check the rack under the table. Inside was a miscellaneous collection of stuff: a small black box in the corner, board games, and literary magazines, to name but a few. He found a towel, took it out, and went over to the south staircase.

The head was still there and he covered it with the towel.

He thought about the chase in the staircase: he'd heard the man unbolting the double-doors, meaning that, at the time, they'd been bolted from the inside.

Ruoping examined them closely. It seemed that all the double-doors in the house were of the same design: they could be bolted from either side, but additionally they could be locked from the outside using a key.

Ruoping recalled that after their meeting about Xiangya's death, he'd left the living room first, and out of curiosity tried the double-doors. They couldn't be opened.

Wait....

Something Lingsha had mentioned occurred to him.

He closed the double-doors and climbed the stairs until he reached the first floor.

He tried the double-doors in the staircase. They wouldn't move.

Ruoping turned and walked upstairs. He went to Bai's study and asked for the key to the double-doors on the first floor.

'What are you going to do?' asked Bai.

'I want to check the forbidden area, the family quarters on the first floor.'

'Want me to go with you?'

'Not good for you. I'll go alone.'

'Okay. Be careful.'

'One question. Did you bolt the double-doors in the south staircase on the ground floor?'

'Yes. To prevent anyone from stumbling into the forbidden area.'

'What about the double-doors on the first floor? I mean the ones opposite the north staircase and the ones in front of the south staircase.'

'Shortly before you arrived I went to my brother's family quarters and bolted the latter set of doors from the inside; after that, I locked those opposite the north stairs from that side, using the key.'

'I see. Last question, do you have spare keys to all the double-doors in this house?'

'No. I should get some made.'

'Good idea. Excuse me now.'

Ruoping left the study and entered the south staircase. He passed by the first crime scene and descended quietly to the first floor.

He was now in front of the double-doors to the forbidden quarters again. Without making any noise, he inserted the key into the keyhole and turned it. The doors were not locked. He pushed hard against them. They were bolted from the other side, just as Bai had told him.

He withdrew the key and went downstairs quietly.

Next, he walked to the north staircase and went up to the first floor again. He went southwards until he reached the double-doors.

He tried the doors using the key. Though they were not locked, they were again bolted from the other side.

The curtains in the corridor were all drawn except for the ones to the right of the double-doors. Ruoping went to the nearest window and looked out. What he saw in front of him was the extension above the recreation room below, consisting of two rooms, the left of which had a window. What lay ahead to his right was the west wing of the house. It was raining hard outside, so he couldn't see anything far away, but he could see that there were three windows along the wall to his left, which was the corridor to which the double-doors led. Only the curtains of the first window were open.

Empty corridors made him think of death and created a sense of hollowness and isolation.

Ruoping shook off his uneasy feeling and turned back.

Soon he was on the ground floor again.

He'd made some progress: a theory had now formed in his mind.

All he needed was proof.

After several hours of searching, Ruoping was back in the living room. It would soon be dinner time. He felt worn out. He hadn't slept at all the previous night and the full day investigation had drained all his energy. Ruoping collapsed into the sofa. A splitting headache made his vision blurry.

'Are you okay, Mr. Lin?'

Lingsha appeared and hastened to his side.

'I'm tired.'

He passed out.

When Ruoping came to, he was still on the sofa, with a blanket covering him. There were two sandwiches and a bottle of milk on the table. Lingsha was sitting on another sofa with a floor lamp beside her, reading a book.

The only light in the living room came from the lamp. Ruoping looked at the clock. Ten past nine.

'You're up,' said Lingsha in her refined demeanour.

'Thanks for staying with me. I really appreciate it.'

'It's dangerous to leave anyone alone, you know.' Lingsha turned her eyes to the food on the table. 'You must be hungry. That's your dinner.'

'Just go back to your room if you feel tired. It's late.'

Lingsha smiled. 'It's not safe if I walk alone back to my room. Take your time eating. I'm reading this novel, and I'll go with you after you've finished.'

'All right.'

He rubbed his temples and started to eat. Lingsha returned to her book, reading quietly.

Ruoping was so hungry he wolfed his meal down.

Lingsha closed the book and said: 'Just leave the dish on the table. Cindy will clear it tomorrow. You are going back to your room, aren't you?'

'Yes, I still have some work to do.'

'Good. Let's go.'

They went upstairs and parted in front of the staircase on the second floor. Ruoping thanked Lingsha again before she disappeared behind the double-doors. She answered with a slight nod.

A remarkably cultivated woman, thought Ruoping.

Back in his room, he took a shower and the fatigue started to recede.

Afterwards, he grabbed his notepad and began jotting a few things down.

He pondered, wrote, and pondered.

At some point after midnight, a flurry of knocks disturbed the stillness of the room.

'Mr. Lin!' It was Cindy.

Ruoping hurried to the door and opened it.

The maidservant was fearful and on the brink of tears.

'What happened?'

'Miss Bai…she's been attacked!'

26 *(Zhengyu Jiang's Soliloquy)*

The door isn't locked, so I just open it and go in.

Cindy will detain Tingzhi. I have plenty of time.

The room is neat: the designs of the bed, the closet, and the bathroom are elegant. There is a small table beside the bed and books everywhere. But this is not the right time to stop and admire.

Wait. Tingzhi is supposed to be in a guest room, but this doesn't look like a guest room. Have I picked the wrong room?

As I look around and think about what to do next, footsteps can be heard outside.

Damn it! If this is not Tingzhi's room then Cindy will be detaining the wrong person. This could be Lingsha's room.

There is no hiding place in the room except the space under the bed. I have no choice!

I turn off the light and slide under the bed.

The floor there is pretty clean. The maidservant must have cleaned the room thoroughly before Lingsha moved in.

The light comes on, casting a beam across the room.

I turn face down slowly and observe from under the bed.

It's Lingsha. I can tell from the way she walks.

Lingsha stands in front of the closet for a moment, turns around, and goes into the bathroom.

I listen quietly. If she takes a shower, that will be a good chance for me to sneak out.

But Lingsha comes out of the bathroom almost immediately. It seems that she was just brushing her teeth. She'd probably taken a shower before dinner.

I curse to myself. If Cindy spoke better Chinese or I spoke better English, I wouldn't have misunderstood her, got the wrong room, and become stuck here.

If Lingsha happens to bend down and look under the bed, it's all over. But that's a risk I'm prepared to take.

Lingsha's feet move back and forth, and then disappear. The bed sinks down a little. Darkness falls. Lingsha has turned in.

She's right above me; there's only a thin mattress between us. My heart beats faster than ever.

I have to wait for the best moment.

I wait in the darkness until I can hear Lingsha's steady breathing. Now is the time.

I move slowly like a snake, crawling out from under the bed without making any noise. The exercise takes me ten minutes....

What happens next is totally unexpected.

As I move towards the door, my right foot hits something. There's the sound of glass breaking on the floor. I've bumped into the small table beside the bed!

The figure on the bed sits up quickly and the light comes on. I stand frozen.

'What are you doing here?' asks Lingsha in great surprise, her hands clutching the quilt.

Words fail me. I turn around and dash towards the door. 'Wait!'

I turn right on the corridor and run. After passing through the double-doors I turn left without thinking.

At the end of the corridor is the public shower room. I turn left again and keep running.

An opening soon appears to the right. I hesitate and go in.

The space is dimly lit. There's a window in front of me; to the right are the stairway and a small room.

As I open the door to the room slightly I change my mind. I decide to go downstairs instead.

My dream has gone to pieces....

Chapter 4
Fall In the Locked Room

27 *(February 12, 12.40 a.m.)*

The room was adjacent to the west staircase on the ground floor.

Everybody was in the corridor beside the room, worried and anxious.

It was Tingzhi who had told the maidservants to wake everyone up.

'Lingsha was in the room,' said Tingzhi. 'I heard her calling for help.'

Ruoping examined the door:

'It looks as though the door has been locked on the inside, just as before…we need the hatchet again.'

Ru and Cindy left immediately.

Ruoping turned to Tingzhi:

'What happened, exactly?'

'Twenty minutes ago, I came downstairs to get some water. As I passed the room here I heard someone groaning and hitting the door feebly from the inside. I tried to open the door but it was locked. A weak voice spoke to me through the door. It was Lingsha.'

'What did she say?'

'She said someone had pushed her downstairs…in the room.'

'In the room? What did she mean?'

'That's all she said.'

Ruoping noticed that Bai was staring hard at Tingzhi, his eyes sad and gloomy.

A couple of minutes later the hatchet arrived. Ruoping took it and began attacking the door.

He already had the knack, so this time it was quickly done. Light streamed out through the crack in the door.

Ruoping put his hand through the crack and unlocked the door.

The room was the same size as the other two, and the same effect was created: stuffiness and dizziness.

Lingsha lay face up, her head pressed against the wall opposite the door. Her arms were spread out and her feet pointed to the door.

There was a small dark pool under her head. From her face, she seemed to have suffered a lot.

Ruoping examined the body but soon realised there was no hope.

'Ling...Lingsha...' Bai stumbled into the room, trembling feverishly.

Ruoping rose and went over to the door. 'Does anyone know why Lingsha was here?' he asked in a flat voice.

No one responded.

'Miss Yan, did you see anyone or notice anything unusual when you went downstairs?'

Tingzhi shook her head.

Cindy and Ru began sobbing. The faces of the others turned sadder than ever.

Bai knelt down beside his daughter with his back facing Ruoping.

It was a surreal moment, thought Ruoping.

Was all this actually a dream created by the murderer?

Death could come at any time. Life was fleeting, but death was eternal. Life was an illusion, but death was the truth.

Lingsha was dead. Her silhouette, as she read her book quietly in the living room a few hours ago, came to his mind.

Ruoping looked at Bai's back. No matter who had committed these ruthless crimes, he would make the monster pay; no matter how clever this devil was, he would beat him in the end.

Although he wasn't a superman, he could strive to be one.

Bai stood up and turned around, his face a mask.

He stumbled out of the room without looking at anyone and disappeared into the darkness.

'Let him go,' said Ruoping. 'Everyone please move to the living room. I'll join you later.'

Soon he was left alone.

Ruoping took a deep breath. He'd been feeling dizzy since he entered the room.

The three deaths had all brought him dizziness. Was it a curse?

There was nothing except a thick layer of dust in the room. No windows.

He bent down, looking at the corpse.

He closed his eyes.

After a moment, Ruoping opened his eyes again. He began examining the body.

There were questions in his mind.

First, Lingsha had been dead for probably less than an hour. The cause of death might be the injury to the head. Lingsha said someone had pushed her downstairs…in the room.

Since he was not a medical expert, he was unable to verify whether she had actually fallen to her death. Nevertheless, he could see there was a severe concussion. He doubted that a mere fall from the stairway could have caused it.

Second….

There was less blood than there should have been. Was Lingsha killed in another place and moved here? But that didn't correspond to her dying message.

So… had she fallen from the ceiling?

Ruoping looked up.

That was ridiculous.

He left the room and closed the door.

Everyone except Bai was waiting in the living room.

It was raining heavily, not only outside, but inside: the rain of silence.

Ruoping investigated everyone's alibi, in vain. Everyone except Tingzhi claimed to be asleep at the time.

According to Tingzhi, after she'd woken up the maidservants, she'd returned to the room in the west staircase and waited.

'You shouldn't have stayed there alone,' said Ruoping.

'I had to, in case anything happened. What's more, I didn't think the killer would strike again within such a short period of time. He would have failed if he'd tried. I'm not as weak as you think.'

'What did you do before we got here?'

'I tried to communicate with Lingsha, but she didn't respond.'

Ruoping turned to the maidservants. 'What did you do after Miss Yan woke you up?'

Ru said: 'I went to inform Mr. Bai and Cindy went to wake up the others.'

Cindy confirmed that Chengyan and Bingyu were both in their rooms when she knocked.

'Did you find Mr. Bai in his room?'

Ru shook her head. 'I couldn't find him anywhere. As I was about to give up, Cindy came and said Mr. Bai was already on the ground floor.'

Ruoping remembered that Bai and the others had joined them shortly after he'd arrived.

Ru continued: 'Cindy said she saw Mr. Bai walking out of the movie room.'

'I see. One more question: had you cleaned any of the rooms where we found the bodies?'

'Only the changing room, but not thoroughly. We haven't even been into the other two rooms.'

'That's all for now. Thank you.'

'Are you finished with your useless investigation?' said Bingyu in his usual scornful tone.

'I'd like to ask all of you for your help,' announced Ruoping. 'Could you please assemble at two-thirty in front of the double-doors opposite the north staircase on the first floor? We're going to enter the forbidden area.'

'What?' exclaimed Bingyu.

'I need you to look for something. I'll let you know what it is at that time. I believe you'll all be surprised by what you're going to find. All right, meeting dismissed.'

As Chengyan was about to ask a question, Ruoping held up a note for everyone to see.

Everyone fell silent.

After he was certain that all of them had understood what was written on the note, Ruoping tucked it into his pocket and left the living room.

28 *(Zhengyu Jiang's Soliloquy)*

I am panting.

I lean against the wall.

Lingsha is dead. I can't believe it. Is this a dream?

I fall to my knees.

Did Lingsha die because of me? But I'd done nothing! All I'd done was hide under her bed....

The fact is that I never saw her again after escaping from her room. I knew Lingsha was chasing me, but that was all I knew. Why did she end up in that strange room?

From what I've learnt by eavesdropping, Lingsha fell to her death. But from where?

I run my fingers through my hair. Am I losing my mind?

Why didn't I feel any sadness when I learnt of her death? All I want to do right now is leave this house.

My dream has gone to pieces. I've just woken up.

I keep listening, and then stare.

I pant heavily as I hear what Ruoping Lin says.

It can't be true. Is the secret already out? Does he already know I've been eavesdropping?

I have to leave now!

Checking my watch, I realise there isn't much time.

I put down the earphone and sort out my stuff in a hurry. I double-check the room, making sure I haven't left any trace behind.

Then I go quickly out of the room.

29 *(February 12, 2.10 a.m.)*

At ten past two, Ruoping, Bingyu and Tingzhi were waiting in front of the double-doors in the south staircase on the first floor.

They leant against the wall, silent. Bingyu seemed impatient and restless, fiddling with the cigarette in his hand. Tingzhi looked calm and composed.

They'd been waiting for over ten minutes.

The two windows in the staircase were both closed. The dim light permeated the stuffy space.

As Bingyu was about to complain, the bolt of the double-doors was pulled back from the other side. The doors parted in the middle and opened.

A young man Ruoping had never seen before stood there.

He seemed to be the same age as Bingyu and the others. The man was thin and had an aquiline nose, pimpled face, and tousled hair. He gawked at them and the yellow suitcase he was holding dropped to the floor.

'Who are you?' asked Ruoping.

'I don't get it!' Bingyu edged forward and shouted. 'Why are you here, Jiang?'

30 *(February 12, 2.15 a.m.)*

In his study, the professor was sitting at the desk with his back to the window.

The only light in the room came from the desk lamp. The laptop screen displayed the email headed *The Identity of the Real Murderer.*

He was near to collapse.

Lingsha was dead. This house was cursed. His family was cursed.

His heart was torn, his tears drained.

Not until he noticed an inconsistency did he realise he could get clues from this email.

Concentrate! It was the only path to the truth! Forget Lingsha's death for the moment!

He stared at the contents of the email.

(5,3)(8,3)(6,1)(5,2)(1,1)(6,2) (8,3)/(6,3)(1,2)(6,1)....

This should be the key to truth...if he could decode this....

The numbers danced crazily in his mind. He tried his best to put them into some kind of order.

He took a pen and scribbled something on a piece of paper.

Negative.

He threw the pen down and clutched his head.

Not in the right direction! Think! Re-navigate!

His mind was in chaos.

Think! Think!

As his eyes ran along the keyboard, a thought struck him.

He paused for a moment before grabbing the pen and scribbling again.

Bingo!

He stared hollowly at the screen, his mind more chaotic and his vision blurred.

Everything before him began swirling around...in the rain.

31 *(February 12, 2.20 a.m.)*

'So you know each other,' said Ruoping.

'Of course!' snorted Bingyu. 'We're all in the same class.'

They were now back in the living room: Ruoping, Bingyu, Chengyan, Tingzhi, Cindy, Ru, and the unexpected guest.

The young man lowered his head, appearing awkward; his trembling hands grasped his knees.

'You said your name is Zhengyu Jiang, correct?' asked Ruoping.

'Yes,' answered Zhengyu feebly.

'He is a recluse,' said Chengyan. 'He's like a hollow man, invisible to everyone.'

'Why did you hide in this house?' asked Ruoping.

'Why...why should I tell you?' Zhengyu's head remained lowered, his voice vague.

'I can speak for you. You're here for someone.'

The young man stirred.

'Just as Chengyan came here for Xiangya, so you're here for someone. You hid on the first floor and spied on us.'

'Spied?' cried Bingyu. 'What do you mean?'

'I mean this.'

Ruoping reached down to the rack under the table, and brought up a small black box.

'What do you think this is?' He put the box on the table.

Bingyu stammered: 'It's a....'

'Bug.' Tingzhi finished the sentence.

'Yes. I believe there's an earphone and related apparatus in his suitcase. I found the other box under the table in the dining room.'

'Dining room?' Bingyu stared open-mouthed at Zhengyu.

'Yes. I suspect he's also attempted to place a third.' Ruoping turned to Zhengyu. 'You'd better tell us what's going on.'

Zhengyu raised his head slowly, his face twisted. He hesitated for a moment before speaking.

'You...you're right. I came here for...for Ling...Lingsha, to whom I gave my heart, although she never knew it.' Zhengyu looked at the floor when he said Lingsha's name.

'So you're the killer!' Bingyu cried, his cigarette dropping from his lips.

'No! Believe me! I didn't kill anyone. I know nothing about the murders here!'

'Perhaps you killed her because your love turned to hatred,' sneered the playboy.

'I swear I didn't do it!'

'He doesn't look like a killer,' said Tingzhi coldly. 'I don't think it's his style.'

Zhengyu winced as Tingzhi made the observation, but he looked away and said nothing.

'I believe you,' said Ruoping. 'Please continue.'

Zhengyu steadied himself and lowered his head again. 'I decided to come here after I discovered that Lingsha had invited Xiangya and others. I knew I couldn't just say I wanted to come along as well because that'd be weird. I'm not anyone's friend. It occurred to me that I could sneak in. The house is huge and there had to be some place where I could hide myself. All I wanted was to be by Lingsha's side, even if she didn't know it. I just wanted to be... an observer.'

There is a certain type of person who isolates himself from the world and is quite content to watch without participating. Apparently Zhengyu was such a type.

'My purpose was to see Lingsha without being seen by her. To achieve this, I thought about getting a—a pinhole camera....'

'You're more perverse than I thought,' sneered Bingyu again, this time with irony.

'I'm not a psycho,' said Zhengyu with pain. 'I just wanted to be a connoisseur of beauty. A connoisseur, you know?'

'Nuts,' said Bingyu.

'I...I finally got the bug but not the pinhole camera. I was content with that, since I could at least hear Lingsha's voice.'

Zhengyu had been avoiding eye contact with his classmates, probably because he knew that, whatever his explanation, it couldn't begin to excuse what he'd done.

'I found the location of the House of Rain from the map and got here by motorbike the day before you arrived. It didn't rain that day, so I arrived safely. I hid my motorbike in the woods and walked to the front door.

'It wasn't easy to get in. I put a yellow bag on the ground several yards from the front door before ringing the doorbell. Then I hid in the corner and waited. My plan was to get in while the person who opened the door went outside to check the bag. Even if the plan had failed, I could have got in through the window using the tool I'd brought with me.'

'Were you a burglar in your previous life?' said Bingyu sarcastically.

Zhengyu ignored the remark and continued: 'Cindy...she came to answer the door.'

'Just as I would have expected,' said Ruoping.

'You seemed to know everything,' said Zhengyu in a trembling voice.

'Do I? Just continue.'

'...This is a lucky coincidence. Cindy worked at my place last year. We're close to each other. When I saw her again I decided to ask her for help. She was surprised to see me, but soon agreed to help me anyway. I didn't reveal my real purpose, and she didn't ask, either. All I needed her to do was find a hiding place and prepare three meals a day for me.'

Cindy lowered her head as Zhengyu continued his story. Ruoping decided not to question her then and there.

'The forbidden area on the first floor became my hiding place, because it hadn't yet been locked at the time I arrived. I moved into the room opposite the room of Lingsha's cousin....

'I went downstairs when everyone was asleep, and put one bug in the living room and one in the dining room. I'd been looking for an opportunity to place a third one in Lingsha's room, but I failed. After the first murder took place, she locked her room every time she went downstairs. I finally gave up trying...I swear I know nothing about the murders, and I know nothing about Lingsha's death.'

Ruoping said: 'So, the mysterious guy I met on the staircase was you?'

'Yes. I just wanted to know what had happened on the second floor...I didn't expect you.'

'I see. Now tell us about your last movements. What prompted you to try again and how did you get the chance?'

Zhengyu bit his lip:

'After learning that two people were dead in such a short period of time, I suddenly had the feeling that it was the end of the world, that all of us were going to die soon in this isolated environment. I needed to be an activist instead of an onlooker. The desperate atmosphere prompted me...so I decided to sneak into Lingsha's room. I decided to do something adventurous like Chengyan.'

Chengyan, who had a faraway look in his eye, said nothing.

'Last night I found Lingsha's room unlocked. I wasn't sure whether she'd be coming back soon or not, but I didn't want to miss the chance. I went in, but she came back unexpectedly. I hid underneath her bed and got trapped.

'I waited until she fell asleep. Then I moved out from under the bed.'

Zhengyu's escape eventually failed. He'd woken Lingsha up.

'Did she chase after you?' asked Ruoping.

'Yes. But I don't know what happened to her.'

'Where did you run?'

'I went downstairs by the west staircase, back to the first floor.'

'Did you notice anything unusual about the room beside the stairs when you were going past?'

'All I know was it was dark inside. When I went past, I thought about hiding there inside the room. I changed my mind as soon as I opened the door slightly.'

'Do you think Lingsha could've noticed that the door was open?'

'I'm not sure. What's the point of this? Are you suggesting that the killer was in that room and killed Lingsha because she intruded into his hideout?'

'Could be.'

Zhengyu sighed.

Ruoping asked: 'Did you notice anything unusual during your stay here? Anything that might shed light on the present case?'

Zhengyu pondered the question. 'On the night of Xiangya's death, I heard something dropping on the floor downstairs while I wandered in the south staircase on the first floor. I went downstairs and stumbled over Xiangya's head. I was horrified. I should have told you about the location of the head because that would have helped you with the investigation. But I couldn't. I didn't want to give myself away. I mentioned this not only because I felt guilty, but also because the shock more or less contributed to the change of mind I just mentioned—.'

'So Xiangya's head is in the south staircase?' Bingyu interrupted.

Ruoping said: 'Yes. I found it too, when I chased Zhengyu down to the ground floor last night. Later I covered the head with a towel. We'd best not move it before the police arrive.'

There was a moment of silence.

Zhengyu broke the ice: 'If you don't mind, I have some questions.'

'Go ahead.'

'How did you know I was hiding on the first floor?'

'Your appearance on the staircase gave everything away. Remember that the double-doors to the south staircase on the ground floor were bolted by the professor. The double-doors to the forbidden area on the first floor were also locked by the professor. Note also that I locked the double-doors opposite the first crime scene after we found Xiangya's body. There are two theories for someone's presence in the locked staircase.

'First, this person might have gone into the staircase before I locked it. He could then have gone all the way down to the ground floor to unbolt the double-doors there, and doubled back. But this theory doesn't work, because after our meeting in the living room following Xiangya's death, I checked the double-doors and they were still bolted from the inside. Furthermore, during the midnight chase, I heard someone unbolting the doors, through which he escaped.

'The second theory, which is the correct one, is that this person had been hiding in the forbidden area before it was locked and then entered the staircase by the double-doors in the south staircase on the first floor. It follows that this person is someone other than one of the guests.

'There are two facts in support of this theory. First, yesterday I discovered that the double-doors at the intersection on the first floor were bolted from the inside, which means that someone had sneaked in and bolted them *after* the professor locked them from the outside using the key. Second, when I examined the same double-doors which opened onto the forbidden area, I found the curtains of the window to the right of the doors were open. Looking through that window, I could see that the curtains of the closest window in the forbidden area were also open. All the other curtains nearby were drawn. That suggested that there might be communication between the two windows.

'Of course, the premises of my entire argument are that the professor didn't lie and that there are no spare keys. Both premises seem to me to be reasonable.'

Zhengyu responded dejectedly: 'Everything you said is correct.'

'No wonder when I questioned Cindy's alibi for Xiangya's murder she appeared uneasy. This was because she was doing your dishes at the time, but couldn't explain why she still had dishes to do at such a late hour. That was why she said she was in the laundry.'

'I…I'm sorry,' said Cindy.

'Don't worry. What you did has nothing to do with the present case.'

Probably to distract everyone's attention from Cindy, Zhengyu said: 'So what you said earlier in the living room was just a trap.'

'Yes. I knew there was a bug in the living room, so I lied. There were only two entrances to the forbidden area on the first floor: the double-doors facing the north staircase and those next to the south staircase. If I asked everyone to assemble before the north doors, the only escape would be through the south doors, in which case all we needed to do was wait there to catch whoever was eavesdropping. Just to be on the safe side, I posted Bingyu, Ru and Cindy at the north doors with instructions to make a lot of noise.'

'But if you made a false announcement how did you expect everyone to understand you?'

'I'd written the real instructions down in advance and showed them to everyone there, right after making the announcement.'

'I see.' Zhengyu sighed. 'Please don't blame Cindy. She's innocent. She never suspected me even after so many people were killed. It's all my fault.' He looked at the girl, whose eyes were still lowered.

'I won't, and the professor won't, either. But what you've done may not be blame-free.'

'I know.'

'I'll explain your deed to the professor…Cindy and Ru, could you please take Mr. Jiang to an empty room to rest? Maybe the one beside the west staircase on the second floor will do. Now, let's return to our rooms and have a rest, too. Remember: don't act alone.'

Zhengyu, in low spirits, followed the maidservants out of the living room. Chengyan, Bingyu, and Tingzhi followed them.

Ruoping remained where he was. He suddenly realised he was contravening his own order, because he had no choice.

Time to think over Lingsha's case.

Again, this was a locked-room murder, motiveless, and with no apparent reason for the locked-room situation. The three murders so far all fell in this same category.

If Lingsha had fallen to her death, where had she fallen from?

One thing he was certain was that Lingsha hadn't fallen from anywhere outside the house, because the body was dry. The only place he could think of was the balcony above the badminton court.

Though a fall from a height of one floor might not be fatal, one could still die by crashing into hard edges or corners on the floor.

He decided to check the badminton court.

Moments later, Ruoping was in the badminton hall. He flicked the wall switch and a weak white light came. It took some time for it to brighten.

He didn't really need to wait to check what he wanted. Standing at the entrance, he raised his head and looked up at the balcony above.

There was nothing unusual on the floor below the balcony. It was made of polyvinyl chloride, meaning that it was almost impossible for anyone who fell onto it to show external wounds.

There were no marks on the green floor except for the white court lines....

So, what was the meaning of Lingsha's dying message?

What she said made sense only if she'd fallen to her death in that locked room.

A body falling from the ceiling—the strange vision kept burrowing into his mind.

PART TWO
SOLO IN THE RAIN

Chapter 5
Death Comes as the End

32

A sense of despair seemed to suffuse the deep mountains.

Bathed in the dim light, Ruoping stood beside the window in his room, looking out.

Though he could barely see the rain, he could hear it.

The faces of the three victims appeared in the hazy air, rotating like a Ferris wheel.

Three were dead, the rest had now been left stranded.

One person among them transcended physical and moral laws; this person aspired to be God. This person wore a mask.

He saw Lingsha's face again. Her words sounded in his ear again.

Fell in the locked room....

Something Tingzhi had said suddenly sprang to mind.

A thought struck him. One piece of the puzzle had snapped into place; there were more to fit in.

Could it be that....

Ruoping turned to look at his cell phone being charged on the bed.

It said seven-thirty.

He left the room.

All the curtains along the corridor were drawn. The omnipresent dim light created a blurred space.

Although it was officially dawn, it was still dark outside.

He turned right when he reached the north staircase and right again in front of the double-doors.

He was now in the west wing of the house, where he could see: the public shower room, an empty room, Zhengyu's room, the west staircase, Tingzhi's room, Xiangya's room, and finally Yunxin's room.

The curtains of the window at the end of the corridor were parted. The grey darkness outside contrasted with the dim yellow light inside.

He went to Tingzhi's room and knocked at the door.

No response.

He knocked again.

The only sound was the rain outside.

Ruoping knocked harder but there was still no response.

He grasped the doorknob and turned. It was locked.

'Miss Yan! Miss Yan!' he cried.

Ruoping turned and scurried back along the corridor. Soon he was back in front of the central double-doors. He pushed them open and hurried to Bai's room.

'Who is it?' came Bai's voice in response to Ruoping's knock.

'Ruoping Lin.'

'Just a moment.'

The door opened to reveal the professor in a white jacket and sports trousers.

'What is it?'

'Sorry to bother you. I know it's pretty early, but I found something important, something that may shed light on Lingsha's case.'

Bai stared at him. His face was wan and battered, as if it had been burned by the blazes from hell.

'You have something?'

'Yes.'

'Actually, so have I.' The eyes in the battered face suddenly became alert. 'We should talk to Tingzhi Yan.'

Ruoping met Bai's gaze, and then nodded.

'I tried her door but it's locked. I need the key.'

'It's in the study. Wait here.'

Looking at the professor from behind, Ruoping felt a surge of sympathy. Lingsha's death must have been a crushing blow to Bai. It was amazing that, in such a miserable state, the professor's mind was still working...his determination to find the killer was unusually strong.

Bai produced a bunch of keys and they returned together to Tingzhi's room. Bai selected the right key and inserted it in the keyhole.

The door was unlocked. It was a normal cylinder lock.

As Bai pushed the door he frowned.

'What's wrong?'

'There's something heavy behind the door.'

'Let me try.'

Bai stepped aside. Ruoping pushed the door with all his strength but could only move it one inch inwards.

'Need my help?'

'No. It's easier to do it singly, as there's not much room to apply pressure.'

Ruoping tried until he became tired. Bai came forward and said: 'My turn.'

They took turns and eventually there was enough space for one person to squeeze in. Bai passed through the narrow space and disappeared from sight.

'Ah!' exclaimed the professor.

Ruoping squeezed into the room in turn. He soon saw that a long bench and a bed, placed side by side, were blocking the door.

There was a desk in front of the window on the west wall. Tingzhi was slumped over it with her back to the door and her ponytail hanging from the back of her head. In front of her on the desk was a laptop showing a Word application. To the right of the laptop were a water bottle, a cup and a wrinkled piece of wrapping paper.

Bai stood beside the desk and stared at the lifeless figure. Ruoping stepped forward and examined the girl.

She was already dead.

33

Mr. Ruoping Lin,

What has happened in the House of Rain during the past two days must be a nightmare for everyone. Why have there been so many deaths? Everything has a reasonable explanation. The present case is no exception.

In fact, the main suspect for last year's case—Weiqun Yang—was my uncle. He brought me up, and was like a father to me. People said he was a devil and a necrophiliac. They were completely wrong.

No one is absolutely evil or good. Perhaps my uncle did some bad things, but he was a good father.

Although there was no direct evidence against him being the murderer, he was made a public enemy. Believe it or not, public opinion was manipulated by one person—Renze Bai.

Bai is a renowned and influential intellectual; what he says carries weight. He convinced the public into believing that my uncle was a beast. The result was that my uncle couldn't sustain the stress and committed suicide.

I understand Bai wanted to avenge his family. But he should have shown better judgment. He accused my uncle of being the killer without any evidence. That was no different from murder.

Though I had lost my uncle, I was still financially secure because other relatives supported me. This gave me enough space to re-investigate the case.

It was not easy. Though I collected all the data I could find, it was all second-hand information. I contacted the police but they didn't help because I was not authorized to know more. I felt frustrated after several months' efforts.

There was still hope. I was surprised to learn that my classmate Lingsha was Jingfu Bai's niece. When she invited Xiangya over I saw a chance to get into the House of Rain. I might find more clues there. I was lucky that Lingsha allowed me to come along, even if we were not close friends.

Before I came here I did one more thing. I sent an anonymous email to Bai with the photos of the crime scene, which I obtained from an underground website. My intention was to make him reconsider the case. I had heard that after my uncle's suicide he had begun doubting his judgment. My move worked. Bai asked you to re-investigate the case. This was the result I expected, as I would have one more person doing the job for me.

You might wonder what the code in the email is. It's my name in coded form. I devised the puzzle out of sheer intellectual satisfaction.

Each of those who came here with Xiangya seemed to have their own purpose. At first I felt they were standing in my way, but I soon realised I could use them.

When I saw Bai I felt upset. He "murdered" my uncle. He was a hypocrite. But I couldn't reveal myself. I had to remain calm.

I felt jealous when I saw Bai talking to Lingsha intimately. That kind of affection was missing from my life. I felt an urge to kill Bai. But that would not have been revenge. Revenge was to let him feel the same pain I had suffered: take his beloved away from him.

The person that mattered most to him was Lingsha. What would he look like if she died? But I couldn't kill Lingsha first, for that might betray the connection between Bai and me. The smartest way would be to kill people for whom I have no motive....

My classmates meant nothing to me. Killing them was like killing ants. I chose Xiangya and Yunxin as the victims, because they were the least intelligent among them. I didn't want to waste my time on Bingyu and Chengyan: they are just rubbish and not worth the effort.

The storm came just in time, giving me time and space to execute my plan.

After Lingsha died, Bai looked like a dead man. I felt joy. But soon I felt empty.

Humans perish so easily. So then what's the meaning of life? Do I live just to take revenge?

In newspapers or stories we often read about the killer leaving a death note before committing suicide. Now I understand perfectly how they feel.

When I went by the stockroom I took some rat poison. I'd made a decision.

You're a detective, so I decided to let you know my story. If you have doubts about what I said, check my suitcase and you'll find documents I collected for this case, which are evidence of what I said.

Tingzhi Yan

Bai turned away from the laptop before Ruoping had finished reading.

'Is what she says about you true?' Ruoping asked.

Bai looked at the south wall. Ruoping noticed that there was a round pillar in front of the wall, connecting the floor with the ceiling. This seemed to be the regular design of the guest rooms in the west part of the house.

'It's true,' said Bai.

'This looks like suicide, but....'

'But?'

'She doesn't mention how and why she committed the impossible crimes.'

'Criminal minds are hard to understand.'

Ruoping didn't reply. He turned to look for Tingzhi's suitcase. It was in the corner. Beside it was a black case for the laptop.

Ruoping bent down and opened the yellow suitcase. There was a red folder. He took it out and opened it.

It was filled, as Tingzhi had said, with documents about the murder case last year, including newspaper clippings, magazine copies, and printed information from the internet. There was also a notebook recording her investigation and random thoughts. The last page had been torn off.

Ruoping put the folder back.

He noticed a quilt had been placed folded on the floor; the folds revealed some part of the quilt which was stained red.

He unfolded the quilt. There was a smell of blood.

Ruoping folded the quilt and straightened up.

'What's that?' asked Bai.

'I suspect it was used to wrap Lingsha's body, to avoid leaving her blood on the floor.'

'What do you mean?'

'I suspect that the room where we found the body was not the crime scene, because there was not enough blood there. The murderer must have wrapped her up in this quilt and moved her there.'

'I...I'm really tired. I'd better go back to my room and take a rest.'

'You should. I'll stay here.'

Bai nodded and squeezed past the bench to leave the room.

Ruoping looked around.

The wooden bench was right behind the door, with most of the bed close against it. The pillar was not far away from either. The window above the desk was locked from the inside, the curtains open. What was unusual about the window was that the lock was sealed with adhesive tapes. The window in the bathroom was in the same state.

There was a small hole on the window frame above the right side of the desk.

He turned his attention to the body.

The girl's head was pressed against her right arm, her left hand curled up on the desk; there was a blue mouse pad on the right side of the laptop.

Ruoping examined the cup and the water bottle, both of which were regular items in every guest room.

The bottle was empty, whilst there was a little water in the cup.

The wrinkled piece of paper beside the cup... that was probably the wrapping paper for the rat poison.

As he examined the north-facing partition forming the north wall of the bathroom, he found something.

On the floor in front of the wall there were two small square imprints, presumably left by the legs of the desk. He checked the space under the desk; there were two more prints.

Which seemed to imply that someone had moved the desk along the west wall of the room.

At first glance, the person who had committed three murders had herself committed suicide and left a death note. Case closed.

But some questions remained. First, Tingzhi hadn't explained how she'd committed the impossible crimes. Second, the state of her room was odd. Why had she bothered to push the bench and the bed to bar the door? And why had she wrapped the window locks with adhesive tape? It seemed to suggest that someone had tried to create the impression of suicide. Finally, he was not really convinced by the death note, which seemed affected, especially the part about why she killed her classmates.

But that was all guesswork.

Suppose this really was another impossible murder: how had the murderer got out of the room? If he'd escaped through the door then how had he managed to move the bench and the bed from the outside? If he'd escaped through the window how had he wrapped the lock with adhesive tapes from the outside?

Four locked room murders and no clues.

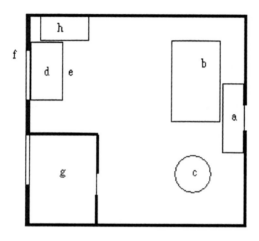

Figure 4.   Tinghzi Yan's room

(a)wooden bench (b)bed (c)pillar (d)desk (e)body (f)holed window frame (g)bathroom (h)closet

Tingzhi's image appeared in his mind.
A confident, calm, smart girl….
A thought came to mind and he froze.
Ruoping looked at the desk again for a moment.
A chill ran down his spine.

34

The figure walked into the garage, took down the raincoat hanging from the wall and put it on.

It pulled the hood of the raincoat over its head, took off its shoes, and put on the waterproof boots. Then it pressed the button on the wall to open the door of the garage.

It was eight o'clock in the morning. The sky was grey.

The figure walked out of the garage in the rain and turned north, keeping its eyes on the ground.

After walking for a short distance the object it was looking for came into view.

The figure picked it up and walked westwards into the woods.

It stopped in a small clearing, bent down, put the object on the ground, and started digging a hole with its gloved hands.

It didn't have time to dig a deep hole. A shallow one was enough. Moreover, even if this was found, no one would realize it was used as the prop for the impossible murder.

The figure buried the object and erased all traces of digging.

It went back to the garage.

Taking off the raincoat and boots, it put its everyday shoes back on.

The figure opened the door leading to the corridor and entered quickly.

35

Due to the incident earlier that morning, breakfast began late, at eight-thirty.

Bai didn't show up. He had told the maidservants to send his breakfast to his room.

'Someone isn't here,' observed Chengyan.

'You're talking about Tingzhi.' Ruoping put down his sandwich.

'Who else could I be referring to?'

'She committed suicide.'

There was consternation among those present. Someone jumped up and a chair was pushed back.

It was Zhengyu.

'Is it true?' he asked in his flat voice.

'Please sit down. I'll explain.' Ruoping could see that everyone was surprised by the man's sudden outburst.

'Is it true?' repeated Zhengyu.

'Just sit down,' repeated Ruoping.

The young man sat down slowly.

Ruoping explained what had happened.

'So it was her!' snarled Bingyu. 'She did look like a cold-blooded murderess!'

'Could the suicide have been faked? Maybe it was another trick!' said Chengyan.

'Don't be so stubborn,' retorted Bingyu. 'You're asking for trouble.'

'But....'

Ruoping paid no attention to their argument.

Soon he was left alone with Ru, who began cleaning the table.

'Excuse me,' said Ruoping. 'I have a question. Is the rat poison kept in the stockroom?'

'Rat poison? Yes.' Ru seemed confused.

'Could you show me?'

Ru nodded. 'Please come with me.'

The stockroom was the second room to the right side of the north staircase. Inside were many cupboards and shelves, holding a wide variety of goods.

Ru opened one cupboard and pointed to a stainless silver can. 'That's it.'

Ruoping took out the container and removed the lid, which had the word "TEA" printed on it. Stacked inside were round lumps wrapped in white paper like tasty pastry.

Ruoping put the can back. 'Since when has it been kept here?'

'All I know is that it was here when we moved in.'

'Thank you. That's all I wanted to know.'

Moments later Ruoping was in the movie room.

The room was magnificent. He'd been longing for a home theatre like this in his own home.

After looking around, something on the shelf caught his eye.

There were a number of boxes inside, along with the English learning materials. He opened one of them. There were four DV tapes inside with white stickers on them indicating dates of recording.

He checked the other boxes. There were twenty-seven tapes in total. He suspected one was missing but he might have been wrong.

Ruoping found the camera and played the tapes one by one.

Somehow he felt thrilled with what he saw.

The individual recording the scenes never showed himself. He or she just walked around randomly. The deathly silence of the scenes imparted a dread chill.

Ruoping put the tapes away.

He decided to get back to his room and gather his thoughts.

After taking a shower, he threw himself on the bed.

He'd had one snowbound case a year ago. The case had taken place at a villa owned by a renowned mystery writer who had been shot dead and had himself become the victim in the puzzle. He'd solved the case before the police arrived. Luck had been with him then, but perhaps not now.

Man is not God. He who aspires to be God is bound to fail. One can never be omnipotent. Anyone who thinks they are, is just betraying their ignorance, for the alleged omnipotence is just child's play from God's perspective.

But one need not be God to solve a murder case.

Ruoping sat up, catching a glimpse of a group of ants in the corner of the wall. They were moving along in a neat order.

Out of sheer curiosity, he pushed one ant out of the parade with his forefinger. The rest went into panic and went in all directions.

He gazed at the ants for a moment. Somehow this scene triggered some vague thought in his mind but it was still too elusive to be captured.

Ruoping lay down again.

His thoughts went back to the case.

There had been seven deaths in this house altogether, and he wasn't even sure whether the first three were connected to the present case.

Maybe he should re-examine last year's case.

He sat up and grabbed his notepad.

Yinghan Qiu: strangled to death by bare hands. Jingfu Bai: hacked to death with a hatchet. Yuyun Bai: strangled to death with a fishing line.

Weiqun Yang had been the main suspect. He'd come to the house that night to meet Yinghan Qiu. At some point he'd gone downstairs to get his cell phone and Jingfu Bai had seized the opportunity to get in and kill his wife. What happened next was a mystery.

Yang maintained that, when he'd gone back to the room again, the entrepreneur and his daughter were already dead. What he'd done was to beat Bai's head with the hatchet, rape the girl's body and take her pendant.

There were three things going against Yang. First, after he'd escaped, no one had been seen getting in or out of the house. Second, given what Yang had done, it was tempting to think that he was capable of murder. Third, given his affair with Yinghan Qiu, he'd had a motive to kill Jingfu Bai, and might well have killed Yuyun Bai because she'd witnessed the murder.

The theory that the entrepreneur had been killed because he'd caught the adulterers on the spot was untenable; in that case the murder weapons should have been things readily handy in the room. But the theory that Yang had planned the murder and prepared the weapons in advance was also questionable for three reasons. First, he would have prepared his own weapon instead of using things from the stockroom; second, it is doubtful that Yang would know the location of the weapons actually used. Third, Yang had met Qiu that night because he knew Jingfu Bai was away. Such being the case, it was baffling that he'd be planning to murder Jingfu Bai.

Suppose Yang had seen Jingfu Bai returning to the house after he'd gone downstairs to get his cell phone. He might have decided to kill

Jingfu Bai on the spur of the moment. But that still didn't explain how he'd known where those weapons were.

Ruoping suddenly thought of the email sent to the professor. That email had arrived not long before the present case had taken place. If the sender was the killer, what was his purpose? If Jingfu Bai's case was connected to the present one, why were Xiangya and Yunxin killed? They'd had no connection to the House of Rain.

Suppose Yang hadn't committed the crime imputed to him? Suppose further that Xiangya and Yunxin had happened to know the identity of the real killer, which was why they were killed. That theory would imply that the real killer was a resident of the house. The only candidates were Lingsha and her father, and the former had also been killed.

That line of reasoning didn't look very promising.

The truth remained to be discovered.

Ruoping was awakened by knocks at the door. It was lunch time.

He went downstairs and finished his meal quickly. Bai was still locked in his study and didn't show up. No one talked during the meal, and soon Ruoping was left alone with the maidservants, who cleaned up after everyone.

He decided to re-examine the third crime scene.

A minute later Ruoping was there. He really didn't want to see Lingsha's body again, but he needed more clues if he wanted to solve the case. He adjusted his mood and then opened the door.

The light was still on; he didn't turn it off when he left the room.

Something suddenly struck his mind.

Wait....

There was a *pattern*— he'd noticed a pattern in the three crime scenes. He looked at the floor closely.

Yes. That was *clever*. Way too clever! It had escaped his eyes!

At last, Ruoping saw the light. Everything came together at once.

To confirm his theory, he put out his hand.

It was late in the afternoon when Ruoping came back from Tingzhi's room.

He'd also checked the other rooms on the west side of the second floor. They all had the same layout in the sense that there was a pillar close to the south wall. He didn't know what architectural purpose it served. Maybe it was just Shengfeng Shi's peculiar taste.

He drew a rough plan of the room in his notepad.

The original state of Tingzhi's room should have been as the plan showed. Yet the desk, bed and bench had all been moved.

The last two had been moved to block the door, but what was the purpose of moving the desk?

He pondered for a moment, then left the room to go to dinner.

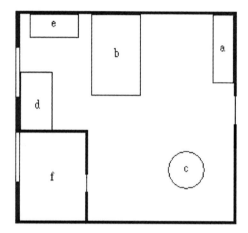

Figure 5. Guest room on the west side of the second floor

(a)wooden bench (b)bed (c)pillar (d)desk (e)closet (f)bathroom

36

Ruoping arrived early at the dining room because he wanted to confirm something with Ru.

Cindy was also there, preparing dinner. Ruoping let her work and took Ru aside.

'Excuse me. I have a question.' He took out his notepad.

'Yes?'

'Did you clean Miss Yan's room before she arrived?'

'Yes.'

'Was the layout of the room like this?' He showed her the plan he'd drawn.

Ru studied it and nodded. 'Yes.'

'Thank you. That's all I wanted to know.'

Dinner was overshadowed by silence again. Bai still didn't show up; he'd been locked in his study all day long.

As dinner came to end, Ruoping broke the silence:

'Ru, could you ask the professor to come here? Please tell him to bring a book for me: *The Detective Stories of Edgar Allan Poe*. I saw this book on his bookshelf. Please go with her, Cindy.'

'Of course.' Ru put down the dishes she was washing and went out of the dining room with Cindy.

'What are you up to?' asked Bingyu, suspiciously.

'You'll see.'

'Let me guess…you've solved the case?' said Bingyu sarcastically.

'As a matter of fact, yes.'

The other stared at him. Chengyan and Zhengyu stopped eating and looked up.

'You…you know who did all this? Not Tingzhi?' asked Bingyu in disbelief.

'Yes and no.'

'Who? Me?' Bingyu burst out laughing.

'No. Not you. I'll explain after the professor shows up.'

'Are you kidding? Are you serious?'

'I'm serious. Now, no more questions until the professor arrives.'

A few minutes later Bai came in with the maidservants. He was no longer the amiable scholar Ruoping had met two days ago. He now looked like someone who'd been to Hell and back.

'What is it?' asked Bai in a lifeless tone, holding the book Ruoping asked him to bring. 'And what's this book for?'

'Please have a seat first.'

Bai showed surprise on seeing Zhengyu. 'Who is this man?'

There was no wonder the professor asked the question. He hadn't been there when Zhengyu had been exposed by Ruoping, because he'd been locked in his study, following his daughter's death.

'He is Lingsha's classmate,' said Ruoping. 'Let me explain.'

Ruoping told him Zhengyu's story. The more he said the more Bai frowned and the more Zhengyu hung his head.

'This fellow appears suspect!' said Bai.

'On the face of it, yes. But he's actually irrelevant to the case.'

'Is he?'

'Yes, because I know everything.'

Silence descended over the dining room.

Ruoping pushed aside his dish and said:

'If you don't mind, I'm going to talk now: talk about the case....'

Chapter 6
Crime by the Divinities

37

All the curtains in the dining room had been drawn. There was a dark shadow inside.

'Interesting,' said Chengyan. 'What's your solution?'

'Wait. I have some questions before you begin,' said Bingyu. 'Does the killer intend to kill some more?'

Ruoping shrugged. 'That's not an appropriate question.'

'What do you mean? Is he here with us?'

'Nor is that.'

'Are you kidding?'

'The truth is beyond your expectations. Are you ready for it?'

'Just tell us.' Bai leaned back in the chair.

Ruoping surveyed everyone before he began:

'There have been four deaths since we came here. But the last one was different from the rest.'

'Different how?' asked Chengyan.

'On the surface, Tingzhi's death was suicide: a death note, door and windows barred from the inside. But it wasn't suicide. It was murder.'

Ruoping's words caused a small commotion, as if everyone was afraid that the killer was sitting next to them. Though most of them didn't truly believe the last case was really a suicide, believing so was psychologically comforting because that would mean the nightmare was over.

'The following reasons support my claim,' continued Ruoping. 'First, if Tingzhi hadn't wanted to be disturbed, she could have simply locked the door from the inside. Why bother moving furniture and sealing the window locks with adhesive tape?

'Second, Tingzhi's water bottle was empty, yet there was water in the cup. Recall that she told us that she'd found Lingsha calling for help when she'd come downstairs to get some water. If she eventually didn't get any water then where did the water in her cup come from?

'Third, Tingzhi wrote in her last words that she'd found rat poison in the stockroom. The strange thing is that the rat poison is kept in a canister marked "TEA." How did she know that it contained rat poison instead?

'All this suggests homicide, and the third point implies that the killer is normally resident here in the house. Also, to fake the death note the killer had to know many details about Jingfu Bai's case and the fact that the professor had received a strange email. Only one person fits all those conditions. This same person tricked Tingzhi into drinking the poisoned water and thus faking the suicide.'

Ruoping turned towards one of the people in the room.

Renze Bai.

Bai remained expressionless.

'That's all guesswork. You haven't any evidence. What's more, I haven't got a motive.'

'You do indeed have a motive.'

'What is it?'

'You thought Tingzhi was the killer. That is, you thought she killed your daughter.'

'Nonsense! Why should I think that?'

'Because you noticed there was something wrong with Tingzhi's testimony.'

Silence.

Ruoping continued:

'There were two inconsistencies in her testimony. First, she said that she'd come downstairs to get water. But she didn't have a water bottle with her! She was apparently lying about why she'd come downstairs.

'Second, she said that Lingsha hit the door feebly and called for help. This means at that time Lingsha must have been just behind the door. Yet when we found her body she was right up against the wall opposite the door. Even if she'd crawled back after speaking to Tingzhi, there should have been a trail of blood or something like that, but there wasn't one. These two inconsistencies prompted me to draw the conclusion that Tingzhi might have lied to us.'

Ruoping looked at Bai. 'You drew the same conclusions and decided to avenge your daughter. Hatred caused you to make a careless judgment. The desperation of this isolated environment, the

150

bloody murders, and the loss of your beloved…all these things caused you to lose your mind.'

Bai was like a statue now. He didn't even blink. The others held their breath and stared at Bai.

Ruoping said: 'One last thing that made you firmly believe your own conclusion is the code in the email you received. You managed to decode it, didn't you? You re-examined the email after you had doubts about Tingzhi, and you suddenly saw the light.'

Ruoping opened his notepad to a particular page and placed it on the dining table for everyone to see.

Q	W	E	R	T	Y	U	I	O	P
A	S	D	F	G	H	J	K	L	
Z	X	C	V	B	N	M			

Code: (5,3)(8,3)(6,1)(5,2)(1,1)(6,2) (8,3)/(6,3)(1,2)(6,1)

Figure 6. English keyboard and the code

'The table I drew here matches the English keyboard for computers. And the code in the email is as shown below the table.

'Now take these ordered pairs as coordinates and the slash as the separating sign.' Ruoping marked the table with numbers.

	Q	W	E	R	T	Y	U	I	O	P
3	Q	W	E	R	T	Y	U	I	O	P
2	A	S	D	F	G	H	J	K	L	
1	Z	X	C	V	B	N	M			
	1	2	3	4	5	6	7	8	9	10

Figure 7. English keyboard as coordinates

'Decode it and you'll get this—Tingzhi Yan!' Ruoping looked at Bai. 'This discovery prompted you to equate the sender of the email with the killer. So you murdered her.'

'Enough. It's time to tell the truth,' said Bai with bleak eyes. 'After losing Lingsha I have nothing. I don't know what's wrong with this house. It's cursed. Rationality and order have been destroyed. Reason escaped me. Everything is twisted in the rain.'

Ruoping didn't reply. He waited for Bai to continue.

'Actually I witnessed Tingzhi behaving strangely. That's why I was more sensitive to the inconsistencies in her testimony.

'In the early morning I was on my way to the movie room to get some stuff. I took the west staircase. As I was approaching the first floor I saw someone in front of the room next to the staircase. I hid quickly and watched. It was Tingzhi, who was making a great effort to drag something wrapped in a quilt. I hesitated about whether I should go back or not. After she went into the room, I seized the opportunity and continued downstairs quickly. A while later I heard the turmoil. I left the movie room and learned of Lingsha's death.

'Not until then did I realise that, when I'd seen Tingzhi earlier, she was moving Lingsha's body. That was mainly what convinced me that she'd killed Lingsha. I didn't know her motive, but that didn't matter.

'What happened afterwards is just as you said. I poisoned Tingzhi and faked her suicide. From her notebook I learned lots of things, including why she came here and why she sent me the email. I was convinced that she'd killed Lingsha out of grudge against me, although apparently she wasn't responsible for the other two murders. Most importantly, from her notebook I also learned the trick of the locked-room murders.'

'You tore that page off,' said Ruoping.

'Yes. Since I used a variation of that trick to create the locked room, I had to tear it off.'

'What else did you take from her room?'

'A DV tape, recorded on the first of February the year before last.'

'Why did you take it?'

'The tape didn't belong to Tingzhi. I just wanted to make the suicide scene as simple as possible.'

'Do you know who made the recording? And why?'

'All I know is Yuyun recorded it to kill time.'

'I have a theory,' said Ruoping to everyone. 'Yesterday morning I found Tingzhi in the movie room. I guessed she'd taken the tape because she'd discovered the key to the impossible murders in it. She'd had a vague idea of trapping the killer using that tape. She formulated the plan after she stumbled over Lingsha's body—I will explain how and where Lingsha died later. She moved the body and deliberately faked the dying message, implying that she knew the trick of the impossible murders. The aim was to frighten the killer into making Tingzhi herself the next target. She planned to set a trap

152

to entice the killer to put his head in the noose. I have to say that she was really brave.'

The man who had killed Tingzhi lowered his head.

'Wait! So what did Tingzhi find about the impossible murders?' said Bingyu impatiently. 'You're talking as if we already know!'

'I'm coming to that. As I revisited the third crime scene earlier I noticed something: the button outside each room and the ones inside are all at the level of an average adult's waist. I searched my memory and soon found a pattern in the first three crime scenes: they have many things in common. First, the rooms are much smaller than a normal guest room in size. Second, next to the door are two buttons inside and one outside the room. Third, the buttons are at the level of an average adult's waist, as I said. Fourth, all three rooms are next to a stairway. These points suggest a hypothesis to me.'

'So what's the point?' snorted Bingyu. 'I don't get it.'

'In everyday life, on what occasion do you see someone walking into a room but find him vanished when the door re-opens? One more hint: people always wait in front of the room for the door to open.'

'I've got it!' shouted Chengyan.

'Yes,' nodded Ruoping. 'The three rooms in question are actually *elevators* in disguise!'

38

'Shengfeng Shi was a genius,' said Ruoping. 'He created an extraordinary illusion. He concealed the truth in every way he could, including the flooring, walls, ceiling, etc. to make the elevators look exactly like normal rooms.'

'Ridiculous!' exclaimed Bingyu. 'You went in and out of those rooms so many times and never noticed?'

'Actually I didn't go in and out many times. And, as I said, I found it the second time I visited the third crime scene. Still, several factors contribute to the illusion. To begin with, we were all deceived by the false first impression. This is a common psychological bias: we judge something we see by what we think it is, rather than what it actually is. Second, not many people actually stepped inside any of the rooms, which made it more difficult to see through the illusion. Third, all the victims died in an unusually terrifying manner, which distracted attention from the room itself. Fourth, the dim light prevented anyone from noticing any architectural peculiarities—such as the groove on the floor which can hardly be discerned without close inspection. The elevators here *don't have safety doors*, so there is actually only one thin groove on the floor. Fifth, the elevators are *silent*: they make almost no noise. Also, don't forget that there were windows near all of the rooms and there was virtually a permanent rainstorm outside; all possible sounds from the elevator would have been covered by the noise of the rain.

'It also explains why each time I entered any of the rooms I felt dizzy. That's what one feels when entering an elevator.'

'But,' Chengyan pointed out, 'if someone had tried to open a door when the elevator was on another floor, then the illusion would've been revealed.'

'Indeed. I think we would have eventually worked it out if we'd stayed here a couple of days longer. But don't forget that all the residents had just moved in, and the maidservants hadn't had time to clean every room in the house.'

'But why did the architect create the illusion in the first place?' asked Chengyan. 'What was the purpose?'

'Purely artistic, I think. Shi was a real artist and it's not surprising he should include some *avant-garde* features.

'Now we know the purpose of the buttons beside the door. They're for the elevators, not for the lights. There is no light button at all in those rooms. If you press the outside one, the elevator will come; the inside ones will take you to the floor you want to go to. The left button is for the lower floor and the right for the higher. So if you're on the ground floor and press the left button, the elevator will take you to the first floor.

'But why are there elevators in the house anyway? Well, the level of the buttons indicate that the elevators were intended for the handicapped—yes, for the professor's father, who passed away shortly after moving in. The House of Rain was intended as a retreat not only for Jingfu Bai, but for his father.

'Now we seem to hold the key to the impossible murders. Let's attempt a reconstruction of the case.'

'Wait!' cut in Chengyan. 'Elevators need monthly maintenance. How can they work after being abandoned for so long?'

'Good question. Remember that the professor mentioned that, before they moved, Shi had come here to do maintenance. The elevators must have been fixed then.

'So, now, let me continue with the reconstruction of the case. Let's call the killer X for now. In the first murder, X presses the elevator button on the ground floor after Xiangya has entered and locked the room on the second floor. The elevator goes down to the ground floor, X enters, kills her, and takes her head—which he throws away in the staircase. Then he presses the inside button on the wall, steps quickly out, and the elevator returns to the second floor.

'In the second murder, after Yunxin enters and locks the changing room door, X presses the elevator button on the first floor. The elevator goes up and he walks in and kills her. Once again, he presses the inside button and leaves quickly. The elevator proceeds downstairs. Simple and efficient.

'In the third case, Lingsha thought Zhengyu had escaped into the room beside the west stairway after noticing the door was slightly open. At that moment, the elevator was actually on the ground floor, which meant that whoever opened the door on the second floor was in danger of falling down the shaft if they stepped in! As soon as Lingsha opened the door, X pushed her down the shaft. Lingsha fell on to the top of the elevator, which had stopped on the ground floor.

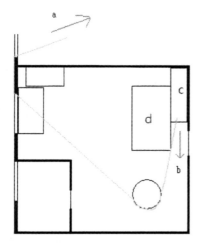

Figure 8.   The trick of Tingzhi's locked room, part 1

(a) the pulling direction of the elevator; (b) the moving direction of the bench; (c) bench; (d) bed

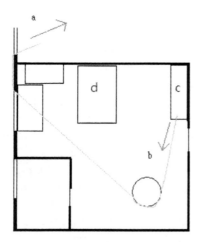

Figure 9.   The trick of Tingzhi's locked room, part 2

(a) the pulling direction of the elevator; (b) the moving direction of the bench; (c) bench; (d) bed

Lingsha's body was soon found by Tingzhi, who was probably investigating the secret of the elevator which she'd learned from the DV tape.

'I suspect my reconstruction isn't entirely correct, but I'll get to that later. The point now is that we have the resources to solve Tingzhi's murder.'

Bai stirred, but said nothing.

Ruoping continued:

'After the murder itself, the killer first opened the window in the landing of the west staircase, which is right beside Tingzhi's room, and brought a length of rope into the room. He fixed one end of the rope to the leg of the wooden bench, circled the rope around the pillar, and pushed it out through the hole in the window frame until it was long enough to reach inside the window he'd just opened. He then returned to the landing and sent the elevator down to the first floor, after which he tied the loose rope to the top of the elevator. He went back to the room again and put the bed and the bench side by side in the corner with the bed slightly more towards the south.

'Then the killer locked and sealed the windows and left the room. He walked downstairs to the first floor, entered the elevator, pressed the ground floor button, and got out. The rope was pulled as the elevator descended and the bench, constrained by the bed, was pulled forward to bar the door.'

Ruoping stopped and turned his notepad to another page on which there was a rough figure showing the mechanism of the trick (see Figure 8).

'The bed had two functions. First, it was used to bar the door to reinforce the suicide impression. Second, without it the bench would have moved in the wrong direction.'

Ruoping turned to the next page showing another figure (see Figure 9).

'When the elevator reached the ground floor, the killer unfastened the rope, returned to the second floor, and pulled that end of the rope back from the first floor. Finally, he tied a heavy article to the loose end and threw the rope out of the window. The first part of the murder was done.

'Now all of you know the murderer is the professor. He had been waiting for a chance to find Tingzhi's body with me present. He would have created one if I hadn't come to him. To complete the whole trick he had to do two more things. First, he had to unfasten the other end of the rope fixed to the bench, after getting into the room. After the rope was unfastened it would be pulled out from the hole because the other end of the rope was attached to the heavy article.

'The reason for moving the desk beforehand was to make sure whoever entered the crime scene would focus on Tingzhi's body and pay no attention to the murderer's unfastening the rope. But it turned out that he did it even before I entered the room.

'The second thing to do was to get outside as soon as possible, collect the rope and bury it.'

'Clever,' commented Chengyan.

Ruoping said to Bai: 'It's amazing that you were able to do all this within such a short period of time. You must have been desperate to revenge your daughter.'

Silence ensued as the audience looked at the battered and gloomy intellectual.

All of a sudden, someone approached the table. Zhengyu was holding a tray of coffee cups. It seemed that he must have left at some point and come back.

'At this stressful moment we need some coffee.' Zhengyu started passing everyone cups, creamers and sugar. He seated himself again after he was done.

No one seemed to care about Zhengyu's unusual behavior. Bai began in a feeble voice.

'Ruoping, please tell me who killed Lingsha. I just want to know the truth. I promise I won't do any more stupid things.'

'You won't be able to revenge your daughter even if you wanted to.'

'What do you mean?'

'There is no way to take revenge.'

'Do you mean…the killer is already dead?'

'The killer is neither dead nor alive.'

'I don't understand.'

'Let's go through this carefully. If X committed the murders as I hypothesized earlier, those who had alibis will be innocent. However, the rest don't have a motive…strictly speaking, no one has a motive.

'Also note that the three murders have three aspects in common. First, they are all impossible murders. Second, there is no obvious reason for creating the impossible situation. Third, all the victims took unexpected moves before they died: in the first case, Xiangya unexpectedly ran into the room beside the stairway; in the second case, Yunxin accepted an unexpected appointment; in the third case, Zhengyu's plan failed unexpectedly and resulted in Lingsha chasing after him.

'There are further curious points in each of the three cases.

'In the first case, why was Xiangya beheaded?'

'In the second case, why did X use Yunxin's scarf as the murder weapon?'

'In the third case, why didn't X move Lingsha's body to prevent us from finding the secret elevator?'

'There's one single answer to all these questions. Once we know it, we know everything.' Ruoping gestured the shuffling audience to silence. 'The key lies in the apparent prescience of the killer. He seemed to know every move the victim would take, so as to perform his murderous trick. As I said, the unexpectedness in each case seems to be inconsistent with carefully planned murders. But no one human can achieve such prescience, so no one could have planned these murders.'

'No one planned the murders...?' asked Bingyu in bewilderment.

'Correct. That explains why we can't think of any reason for creating the impossibilities, because there wasn't one.'

'But if it was murder someone had to plan it!'

'Why should it be someone instead of some other agent?'

'What are you talking about? Are you insane?'

'I've never been more serious.' Ruoping paused for effect.

'The murderer was not human.'

If any member of that audience looked back at Ruoping's lecture a few years later, they would probably regard that moment as the most memorable, for the revelation of the truth was as astounding as the tragedy itself.

'Are you serious?' questioned the professor, looking baffled.

'Of course I am,' replied Ruoping.

'You must be kidding.' Bingyu banged his cigarette box against the table. 'Is the murderer a gorilla hiding somewhere in this house? It must be more intelligent than a magician.'

Ruoping shook his head. 'Your comment contradicts your conclusion.'

'I guess,' said Chengyan, 'The murderer is not even an organism.'

'Correct.'

'Robot? Supernatural powers? This is getting more and more ridiculous!' Bingyu muttered.

'Robot is not an option because current Artificial Intelligence is not smart enough to commit the sophisticated murders we have at hand. Supernatural powers...you're almost right. According to Buddhism, there exist three worlds: the world of desire, the world of form, and the world of formlessness. For the Taoist, the three worlds refer to the heaven, the mundane, and the underworld. Our murderer does not belong to the mundane, so it is not human; it does not belong to the underworld, so it is not a ghost. The only option is the heavens. Actually—its name is...Fate!'

'Our destiny is determined by Fate. We don't have free will; we don't know our destiny.'

'So what? Do you mean Fate was responsible for the murders?' asked Bingyu.

'If you agree that accidents are part of our fate, then yes.'

'Accidents?'

'Yes. Each of the victims died in an accident.'

'I'm beginning to feel,' said Bingyu with an ironic smile, 'that you're more insane than our murderer.'

'How is it possible?' asked Bai.

Ruoping replied: 'Nothing is impossible. People just don't believe that maxim. Let me explain.

'In the first case, the red wine Xiangya drank was prepared by Chengyan, who rejected Cindy's offer to take the wine upstairs for him. When I questioned him, Chengyan's reaction was odd. I found more clues when we played cards together yesterday. Guess what Chengyan was up to.'

'He doped the wine,' said Zhengyu in a flat voice, as if he were the one who had done it.

'Sleeping pills, right?' Ruoping looked at Chengyan, who turned his eyes away.

'No need to conceal this anymore,' said Chengyan after a long pause. 'I pretended to take a sip and she had no doubts....'

Ruoping said: 'Xiangya realised your intention after she started to feel sleepy. That was why she escaped. She ran into the room by the stairway entirely by accident. She was afraid that you'd be able to locate her by the light under the door, so she thought she'd better turn it off. That was when things went wrong. She unwittingly pressed the elevator button for the ground floor.

160

'The elevator went down. Xiangya had passed out shortly after she'd used her last bit of strength to open the door of the "room," and her head became jammed between the edge of the elevator floor and the wall of the elevator shaft.

'At the same time, on the second floor, Chengyan was trying to force the door open. He hit and kicked at it before the professor and I stopped him.' Ruoping turned to Bai. 'I'm not sure whether you still remember, but one of Chengyan's random kicks hit the button beside the door—not surprisingly, since it's at waist-level. So the elevator went up.'

Ruoping took a sip of coffee and continued: 'Recall that the professor mentioned that his brother complained that there were flaws in the design of the house. We thought he meant the doors of the changing room. But actually he meant the flaw in the elevator: the outside door of the "room" can still be opened after the elevator has started moving, which is what caused Lingsha's fall. As I said earlier, the elevators in this house don't have proper elevator safety doors. A normal elevator will move only when its door is properly closed. But that's not the case here in the House of Rain. If someone presses the elevator button at any time, the elevator will start to move!

'That turned out to be deadly for Bai's father. If the elevator button were to be pressed before his wheel-chair was completely inside, the resulting movement could overturn the wheelchair. This was Shi's revenge. Jingfu Bai didn't pursue the matter because his father soon passed away.

'Xiangya was another unfortunate victim of Shi's revenge. She fell unconscious and her head got jammed as the elevator rose and tore it off. As a result, the head fell into the stairwell and was found by Zhengyu and then by me.

'Now we know what possessed the force to tear her head off: it was the elevator.'

'It's my fault,' said Chengyan. 'I caused her death.'

'It's not that simple, and it depends on how you look at the matter. I could argue it was Fate.'

'Wait,' said Bai, puzzled. 'You said Xiangya opened the door before passing out, which means the door of the "room" in the south staircase on the ground floor would have remained open. Why didn't you notice the secret of the room when you found Xiangya's head? The elevator was up at the second floor, so the empty space on the ground floor should have given the game away.'

Ruoping turned to Zhengyu. 'I assume you must have closed the door after you found Xiangya's head?'

Zhengyu stuttered and ran his fingers through his tousled hair.

'Y—Yes. I thought about moving the head into the room but changed my mind. I closed the door without thinking. I didn't turn the staircase light on, so I didn't see there was just an empty space there.'

'That clears things up.'

'What happened in the second case?' asked Bingyu with a mixture of amusement and impatience. 'Was that an accident as well?'

Ruoping replied: 'Yes, that was an elevator accident as well. After entering the changing room, Yunxin locked the door. Then she opened the back door, probably out of curiosity. Her scarf got caught between the frame and the door when she slammed it shut, but she turned round without noticing it. She was probably afraid that the loud noise she'd made would attract the maidservants' attention, so she tried to turn the light off, but actually pressed the button for the first floor.

'The elevator went up and its immense, relentless power strangled Yunxin to death. The scarf was torn apart and one piece of it dropped down outside the house. Several threads got caught in the door-frame. The elevator had killed again.'

Ruoping turned to Bingyu, 'You and Chengyan arrived shortly thereafter. Chengyan suggested you turn off the light to oblige Yunxin to come out, but you didn't realise the reason the light wasn't on was because the elevator wasn't there. When Chengyan pressed the outside button, the elevator returned. A moment later we found Yunxin inside, as dead as mutton.'

'Nonsense!' Bingyu protested. 'I don't believe it a bit! This is just a crazy coincidence!'

Ruoping replied calmly: 'Crazy coincidences occur all the time, all over the world. Before I elaborate, let me explain what happened in the third case, when Lingsha said she fell. That's true, but nobody pushed her. She opened the door and stepped inside without realising there was no floor, because the elevator was at ground level. She fell down from the second floor, and the elevator claimed another victim. These kinds of elevator accidents happen every year all over the world. Just check the newspapers.'

Bai groaned, but he didn't reject Ruoping's theory, probably because he hadn't a better one of his own.

Chengyan shook his head. 'I understand there are elevator accidents. But in this case there are too many coincidences. Have you verified your hypothesis?'

'Yes. I found there's a bloodstain on the ceiling bordering the elevator room in the staircase where Xiangya's head was found. And there's also blood on the top of the elevator in the west staircase, where Lingsha died. As for Yunxin's case, the thread that got stuck in the doorframe is telling evidence already.'

Chengyan sighed. 'If you're right, then I indirectly caused Xiangya's and Yunxin's deaths.'

'And I caused Lingsha's death.' Zhengyu looked at his hands.

'No!' replied Ruoping. 'I know it's hard to accept but I believe this is the truth we have been seeking. There is a causal chain in each of the three deaths. Why did Xiangya black out? Because she was doped. Why was she doped? Because Chengyan put his reveries into practice.

'What about Yunxin? She dressed herself because she was going to meet Chengyan. She probably chose that scarf just for him...then her curiosity, plus that scarf, killed her.

'As for Lingsha's death, Zhengyu's movements were crucial: his hiding in Lingsha's room and his opening the door of the room by the stairway. But don't forget his deed was partly inspired by Chengyan's theft of the car keys.

'All this would not have happened if Lingsha hadn't asked Xiangya over, or, to trace things back to their origin, if Jingfu Bai hadn't built this house and Shengfeng Shi hadn't taken his revenge.'

'Taken separately, each coincidence is acceptable,' said Chengyan. 'But it's almost impossible to swallow when they're all put together.'

'Almost impossible,' smiled Ruoping, 'so it's still possible. Please pass me the book I asked you to bring for me, professor.'

Looking puzzled, Bai handed the book to Ruoping.

Ruoping leafed through the book and stopped at a particular page. 'Edgar Allan Poe in "The Mystery of Marie Rogêt" writes: "There are few persons, even among the calmest thinkers, who have not occasionally been startled into a vague yet thrilling half-credence in the supernatural, by coincidences of so seemingly marvellous a character that, as mere coincidences, the intellect has been unable to receive them." In another paragraph he writes: "The extraordinary details which I am now called upon to make public, will be found to

163

form, as regards sequence of time, the primary branch of a series of scarcely intelligible coincidences...."'

'But,' protested Bingyu, 'you're quoting a fictional text....'

'Let me give you real-life examples. Poe himself is a perfect example of incredible coincidence. His only novel, *The Narrative of Arthur Gordon Pym of Nantucket*, published in 1838, claimed to be based on a true event, in which four survivors of a shipwreck cast away in an open boat drew lots to decide who would be eaten. A cabin boy named Richard Parker became the victim. Forty-six years later, four survivors from a shipwreck in an open boat did the same thing, and the person eaten was also a cabin boy named Richard Parker....

'I could go on... BBC news reported that in Finland, 2002, seventy-year-old twins got killed on the same road in separate accidents within the space of only two hours. The first of the twins crossed the road on his bike and was hit by a lorry. Later the second crossed the same road on his bike and was also hit by a lorry. The police said it was unlikely that the second man would have known of the first's death, and that it's extremely unusual to have deaths on that road within such a short period of time.'

The amateur detective adjusted his silver-frame glasses on his nose and said: 'The ancient Chinese philosopher Laozi once said, "Heaven and earth are not like humans, they are impartial. They regard all things as insignificant, as though they were playthings made of straw." There is an interesting analogy here. When you remove a few ants from a parade, they become completely disoriented and don't know what to do. We're the ants and we are the playthings of a higher being.'

The lecture came to an end. The rain outside had stopped.

Renze Bai broke the silence.

'So, what happened in the past few days is unconnected to the tragedy last year?' he asked in a dry voice.

'That's correct.'

'Is my brother's case now completely solved?'

'That's another story. I'll leave that for another time.'

There were whispers among the audience. The dim light made everything dreamlike. Though the rainstorm had stopped, the shadow in the house had not completely disappeared.

As Bai was reaching to get more coffee, the phone in the living room rang and he sprang to his feet.

'It's the police! They said they'd call again. Let me get it!'
He went quickly over to the phone.
'Hello, this is Renze Bai....'

I can see people's faces relax as they learn that the police will arrive in twenty minutes.

Apparently the murderer of Tingzhi is not going to touch his cup again because they have to prepare for the arrival of the police.

What a shame. A lame duck like me could have done something for Tingzhi.

I saw Ruoping Lin's half-smile when the phone rang. The young scholar could read my mind. Even if the phone hadn't rung Ruoping Lin would still, in some way, have prevented the murderer from committing "suicide."

That detective had known everything, probably from the very moment I'd lied about my purpose for being here.

I could have made myself somebody...somebody in the spotlight, instead of an onlooker in the corner, by committing a murder.

But I know I am forever destined to be a nobody.

EPILOGUE:
SOLILOQUY IN THE RAIN

Dad had left.

From the window at the end of the corridor I could see the blue Porsche disappearing in the drizzle.

My breath made the window filmy. I drew my hands from the window and turned around.

The fluffy red slippers stepped out into the snaking corridor. I turned right at the end of the corridor and kept walking until I saw the double-doors. I opened the doors, walked in, closed the doors and leant back against them.

There was light coming from the room on the left side far ahead. That was Mom's room.

Again, a sense of strangeness seized my heart. I felt like a visitor rather than a resident in this house.

I walked to the first room on the left, opened the door and turned on the light.

This was my room.

Some years ago Dad had spent lots of money building this house. The House of Rain became my new home.

It was a luxurious house. I had everything here and all of my classmates envied me.

I walked to the shelf holding numerous dolls and picked up the little raccoon. It had plenty of patches all over. It was my birthday gift from Mom when I was eight years old.

It was my best friend.

I turned to the desk, on which there were a computer, a laser printer and a scanner. I sat down, opened the pink diary and started writing.

10th February, Rainy

Dad is hanging out with friends. Mom gave the maidservants the day off and they all left happily.

It began last summer. Dad started hanging out once a week, and Mom would give the servants the day off. I soon knew what was happening. Mom was having an affair. His name is Weiqun Yang.

Mom and Dad have fights everyday. They can't even talk normally to each other. I've been living through their quarrels and fights. My dolls are my friends, but my parents' shouts penetrate even the wall formed by my dolls.

I asked Mom why they got married if they don't get along well. She said I was too young to understand. I asked her why they didn't get divorced. She gave me the same reply.

I don't understand.

Dad's affair with the architect's wife was what made my parents' souls separate. From that day on, my happiness was gone.

I get anxious when winter or summer vacation comes, because that means I will need to stay in this hollow house, although I have everything here, except love.

I know Yang will come tonight, because Dad is away. That man will come upstairs quietly and enter Mom's room....

Throwing the pen down, I clutched my head.

Every time Yang came, I would go to the piano room to cry. I would take the little raccoon with me and stay there overnight.

I would play the melodies I'd written on the piano. Only when darkness fell did inspiration come.

For convenience I stored some food and put another set of pillows and a quilt in the piano room. All I had to do then was just take the little racoon with me.

Someone opened the double-doors. There were footsteps.

'You're late.' Mom's voice came. They burst into laughter.

I didn't want to listen to what came after the laughter but the sounds just flooded in, drowning even the sound of the rain.

I stood for a while, and then put down the little raccoon.

Opening the closet, I took out a pair of gloves and put them on.

I opened the door quietly and stepped out.

I remembered there was a hatchet in the stockroom.

I went downstairs from the north staircase, my long hair caressing my face.

The stockroom wasn't locked so I just walked in.

I spent some time searching for the hatchet, my heart beating fast.

There it was.

I carefully wiped the grip using a piece of cloth.

Taking a deep breath, I left the stockroom and went upstairs.

When I was back in front of my room, I heard Mom screaming. It was from her room, the door of which was half open.

'No...no...' The voice trailed away.

My heart beat faster than ever. I hurried to Mom's room and opened the door.

In the dim light there was a man wearing a coat with his back to me. He was kneeling on the bed with his hands around Mom's throat. Her face was twisted in agony.

It happened very quickly. The hatchet in my hand dashed forward. It was a quick blow and the man fell down on the floor. Channelling my hatred, I blindly inflicted more and more blows....

After the man lay dead, the mist cleared from my eyes and I could see who it was.

It was Dad.

The hatchet dropped from my hand.

I stood still.

There was a moment of blankness before my reason returned.

I went over to the bed and examined Mom, whose face was still twisted.

No sign of life.

I didn't check Dad. I was so tired.

Tears welled up in my eyes, and I didn't know whether I was sad or happy.

Yang must have left for some reason, and Dad had come back to catch them. Why did he still care about what Mom was doing if he didn't love her? I couldn't work it out, but I knew the circumstances would make Yang the main suspect, which was a relief for me.

I left the room. Standing in the corridor, a thought came to mind.

I went downstairs again to the stockroom. I took a saw, a fishing line, an empty clothes stand, and some glue. I cut the line into the length I thought appropriate.

Going back to my room, I took the little raccoon with me.

I went to the elevator room in the south staircase on the first floor, opened the door and walked in.

I placed the clothes stand with its round base facing the door, put one end of the fishing line around the base and made a loop. I made the other end of the fishing line into a relatively bigger loop.

Next, I stood the saw horizontally and glued it to the floor between the stand and the door. I left the room and threw the glue and the gloves in the study.

Going back to the elevator room, I pressed the second-floor button. Just before the elevator started to move, I pulled the fishing line over the edge of the saw and then out of the room.

I closed the door, pulled the fishing line from under the door and put the loop around my neck. With my back leaning against the door I sat down.

The elevator was going up. The base of the clothes stand, fixed to the fishing line, would be pulled to press the saw against the door and then the wall. The fishing line would eventually be cut by the saw as the elevator kept going up and pulled the line.

The trick might fail but I was going to try my luck. I held the little raccoon tightly, as the loop around my neck became tighter.

Yang would soon become the main suspect. There was a chance the police would find the secret of the elevator and see through my trick, but that would depend on Fate.

I was overcome by pain. The little raccoon dropped from my grip.

The last thing I heard was the sound of rain, mixed with the melody I had composed.

The melody of a dirge.

AFTERWORD

As stated in the Foreword, Szu-Yen Lin is one of the rising stars of Taiwanese detective fiction, whose short story, "The Ghost of the Badminton Court," won first prize in the second Werewolf Castle Mystery Literature Award in 2014 and subsequently became one of the first Chinese-language stories to appear in *Ellery Queen's Mystery Magazine (EQMM)* in August of the same year.

So far, he has published eight novels: *The Nile Phantom Mystery (2005), Death in the House of Rain (2006), The Ice-Mirror House Murders (2009), The Curse of Pattaya (2010), The Nameless Woman (2012), The Night of the Mask (2013), The Maya Mission (2014),* and *The Tear Collector (2015).* Not all feature impossible crimes. He has also published three short story collections: *The Fog Villa Murder Case (2014), Ruoping Lin's Solution (2016), Ruoping Lin's Worry (2017).* In May 2016, "The Miracle on Christmas Eve" was the second of his stories to appear in *EQMM.* His series detective, Ruoping Lin, is a philosophy professor; Szu-Yen Lin himself holds a doctor's degree in philosophy.

Death in the House of Rain is the most Carr-like of his novels, with overtones of *Grand Guignol,* the legendary Paris horror theatre. However, its most striking feature is the peculiar architecture of the building, and here the mystery falls into the Japanese *honkaku* camp.

Honkaku, or more precisely *shin honkaku,* since its renaissance in the 1980s, follows the same rules of fair-play as the western Golden Age style of the 1930s, but with a determination to test the limits (such as use of narrative tricks mentioned in the Foreword).

Architecture of a special shape and structure is another example of *honkaku* pushing the bounds. We cannot think of an instance in western detective fiction, but the *new honkaku* school has many examples: Shimada Soji, Yukito Ayatsuji, Kitayama Takekuni, Kirisha Takumi, Abiko Takemaru and Utano Shougo have all written at least one such mystery. Sometimes, the special structure of the architecture is necessary to the execution of a seemingly impossible murder: i.e. but for the trick, the structure of the building makes no sense. Sometimes it serves as a red herring. Just as with any experimental endeavour, reactions seem to be extreme: fans like the diabolical ingenuity made possible by the architecture, whereas others challenge the credibility of building a strange house for the sole purpose of killing someone. In the case of *Death in the House of Rain*, the house is shaped like the Chinese character for "rain". The question posed to the reader is whether that is necessary to the execution of the murders, or merely a diversion?

John Pugmire and Fei Wu

CPSIA information can be obtained
at www.ICGtesting.com
Printed in the USA
LVOW07s1610231017
553452LV00011B/1197/P